She was knowing and affectionate, and so pretty he couldn't resist her. He put a hand on her knee and leaned in to kiss her. Her mouth was soft and willing, and he put down the coffee cup and took her face in both hands.

After a long, intense interval of suspended time, she pulled away and rested her forehead against his. "Oh, Reid," she said—half disapproval, half sighing acquiescence. He stroked her breast, and her breathing quickened, and he slid a hand over her nylon-clad knee and under her skirt to find bare thigh. "Don't," she said.

He paused but didn't withdraw his hand. "Is that no?" he asked.

She sighed. "Not yet," she said, but she was warning him too, not to go too far, beyond the point of no return. Only it was hard to know where that was.

I0598363

Praise for Linda Griffin

"Griffin has a gift for romantic suspense."

~Kirkus Reviews

~*~

"*GUILTY KNOWLEDGE* is an intriguing story…a compelling tale of murder, secrets, and love."

~Moira Wolf, InD'Tale Magazine

~*~

"*THE REBOUND EFFECT* … is a suspenseful psychological thriller that did not disappoint."

~Joanie Chevalier for Readers' Favorite

Love, Death, and the Art of Cooking

by

Linda Griffin

This is a work of fiction. Names, characters, places, and incidents are either the product of the author's imagination or are used fictitiously, and any resemblance to actual persons living or dead, business establishments, events, or locales, is entirely coincidental.

Love, Death, and the Art of Cooking

COPYRIGHT © 2021 by Linda Griffin

All rights reserved. No part of this book may be used or reproduced in any manner whatsoever without written permission of the author or The Wild Rose Press, Inc. except in the case of brief quotations embodied in critical articles or reviews.
Contact Information: info@thewildrosepress.com

Cover Art by *Jennifer Greeff*

The Wild Rose Press, Inc.
PO Box 708
Adams Basin, NY 14410-0708
Visit us at www.thewildrosepress.com

Publishing History
First Edition, 2021
Trade Paperback ISBN 978-1-5092-3777-7
Digital ISBN 978-1-5092-3778-4

Published in the United States of America

Dedication

To the real Alyssa and Jane
and all the nice guys who love to cook

Acknowledgments

I would like to acknowledge my good fortune in being assigned a wonderful editor, Nan Swanson. Thanks also to cover artist Jennifer Greeff and the rest of the Wild Rose Press team.

Chapter One

The irregular layout of the dark, empty streets was confusing, and Reid discovered too late that he had taken the wrong one. He was so intent on his mistake and finding his way back that he didn't immediately register the flashing lights behind him. With a sudden shock he realized he was being pulled over by a police car in an unfamiliar California city.

The officer who approached the window as he rolled it down was about sixty, with round eyeglasses and a white mustache, bareheaded even in January. He leaned in and said, "Evening, sir," in a gravelly voice. "License and registration, please."

"Good evening, Officer," Reid replied, reaching for his wallet. "What did I do?"

The cop didn't answer and, as he studied the license, asked conversationally, "Were you trying to evade arrest?"

"What? No!"

"Didn't make a U-turn as soon as you saw me?" He looked up and smiled. It wasn't a friendly smile.

"Oh, no—I *didn't* see you. I made a wrong turn back there, and I was trying to get back."

"Uh-huh," the cop said. He handed back the license and registration and said, "Please get out of your vehicle, sir."

Reid complied numbly, struggling a little with the

seatbelt. Damned inanimate objects were so contrary. He was a bit lightheaded, but the cool, fresh air felt good. He glanced down the quiet residential street. A single porch light and a few lighted windows were the only signs of life.

The officer pointed to a spot under the nearest streetlight. "Walk over there and back to your vehicle."

"What? Oh, no, Officer—" He leaned closer to read the name tag above the cop's breast pocket. The light was poor, and he couldn't quite make it out. Boetticher? And how would that be pronounced? "I'm not impaired. I only had one drink. I was just lost. I'm new in town."

"Welcome to Carroll City," Officer Boetticher said dryly. He pointed again.

To humor him, Reid made his way to the light post and back. He stumbled a little on the uneven sidewalk but hoped the officer could tell it wasn't a drunken stagger. He wasn't impaired. He was fine.

When he got back, Boetticher said, "Stand right there," and walked back to the patrol car. Reid stood close to the car with one hand on the top to steady himself and waited. The cop must be checking his information against the police database, but when he came back, he had something in his hand. Reid had never seen one before, but he knew what it was—a breathalyzer.

****

The phone was ringing, a shrill interruption in the dark, silent room. Alyssa grabbed for it before she realized it wasn't the cell phone she had left on her nightstand. The landline in the living room would only ring this time of night for bad news. Her mind automatically ran through the list of possible disasters as she rolled out of bed and padded down the hall. The night light next to the end table led her to the phone, and she grabbed the receiver.

"Jane?" a hopeful voice asked. A man's voice, pleasant but unfamiliar.

"No," Alyssa said. "She's not here. Call her cell." She was both relieved that it wasn't her father and annoyed in general.

"I did. I think it's turned off. When will she be home?"

"I have no idea. I'm not her keeper. Call tomorrow."

She was about to hang up, but the voice said, "No, please… I don't have anyone else to call. Do you know where she is?"

"No." She shifted from one foot to the other and brushed hair out of her eyes. "I was asleep, and I'm going back to sleep now."

"Look, I'm very sorry, but… I don't even really know Jane. I don't know anybody in town except the dude I interviewed with today, and he insisted on taking me out for a drink afterward. I swear I only had one drink. The office is closed now, and I don't have his cell number. Jane gave me her card, so… I just need somebody to pay the bail bondsman and maybe give me a ride back to my motel. They won't let me pay the bond myself because I don't live here, and they won't take a credit card for the full bail amount. I'll pay you back right away."

"Seriously? You seriously expect me to drive downtown and bail out a drunk driver I don't even know?"

"I'm not a drunk driver," said the voice. "I'm not drunk."

"Only a drunk would call a stranger in the middle of the night." She didn't understand why she was still talking to him. Her warm bed beckoned.

"I swear to God if you help me, I'll make it up to you."

"Yeah, right. Do you even believe in God?"

"Do I—?"

"What's your name, genius?"

"Re—no, it's Emerson Lucas."

"Are you sure?" She didn't wait for an answer. "How much?"

"Five thousand—so five hundred for the bail bondsman."

"First offense, then? You realize if you skip town I'll have to pay the full amount? What was your BA?"

"Point oh nine."

Alyssa sighed. "Where are you? Downtown? I'll be there in twenty minutes. You and Jane both owe me big time." She hung up before he could say anything to change her mind. This was incredibly stupid, but he had sounded so lost.

****

In the brightly lit jail lobby, she traded pleasantries with the clerk while she signed the necessary papers at the bail window, taking responsibility for getting the miscreant home. The ambient odor was a nauseating blend of unwashed bodies and eye-stinging disinfectant, and she was impatient to be done with the place and with him.

He was about thirty, with slightly shaggy, dirty-blond hair and dark eyes, not what she would call impressive in any way, but apparently harmless, like a cocker spaniel. Not tall, not thin, but chubby would be an overstatement. Not sexy, not her type, not Jane's usual type either. He wore casual clothes, but nice ones: pressed trousers, collared shirt, sweater vest, no jacket.

He wasn't obviously inebriated, but as soon as he saw her, he started apologizing. "I am so sorry. I'm sorry I woke you up and made you come down here. I've never had to do this before—it's so embarrassing." He did look embarrassed, but there was something else in his expression. It wasn't admiration—she was hardly at her best, in sweatpants and a T-shirt and her hair in a sloppy ponytail—but more like surprise, as if he thought he recognized her from somewhere.

"It's supposed to be embarrassing," she said heartlessly. "Get a grip, Lucas."

"Thank you for coming," he said.

Under other circumstances, she might have liked his pleasantly husky voice, but given her interrupted sleep, even his heartfelt gratitude was annoying. "Come on. I want to go back to bed," she said and turned away.

He followed her to the parking lot and her white Chevy Sonic. She unlocked the doors and got in without looking at him. As soon as she was sure he was in, she started the car.

"I'm sorry," he said again. "I didn't know what else to do."

"You could have spent the night in jail," she suggested. She didn't blame him, though. The drunk tank was not a pleasant place, even without a hangover.

"But if you'd seen the guy they put me in with…"

"Afraid he would rape you?" she asked.

"Or give me TB," he said.

"Well, Mr. Lucas, I hope you learned your lesson."

"Yes. My friends call me Reid."

"I'm not your friend." She turned onto the street and asked, "Where to?"

"The Holiday Inn on Western—by the—"

"I know where it is."

"I really appreciate this. How can I make it up to you?"

"You could start by paying back the five hundred dollars you owe me."

"As soon as I can get to an ATM," he promised. "Tonight, if you know where—"

She wasn't going to drive around looking for one. "You can send it to me or give it to Jane. And don't drink and drive again."

"God, I probably won't be able to drive at all for a while."

"Let's leave God out of this," Alyssa said.

"Sorry. Do you know what the fine will be?" Before she could answer, he added, "No, of course you wouldn't."

"Twenty-six hundred," she said. "Point oh nine… A good lawyer might be able to get you off." She concentrated on her driving, but she could feel him watching her. Trying to remember where he had seen her before? She was sure he hadn't. Jane certainly hadn't introduced them. "Did you get the job?" she asked after a moment. "You're going to need the money."

He laughed without much amusement. "I don't know. I think so—if they don't find out about this. The drink was his idea, though. I don't usually drink much at all."

"I've heard that before."

"Yeah, but really. And I will make it up to you. I owe you dinner at least. You and Jane both, of course."

"How did you meet her?"

"It's a long story."

"I bet." She could imagine—Jane liked bar hopping. Even though he wasn't her type, Alyssa could easily imagine their encounter had ended in bed. "I appreciate the thought, but I don't want to go out with you, with or without Jane. Nothing personal."

"No, I meant I'll cook dinner for you. I'll have to use your kitchen, though."

"Do you know how to cook, or is that promise in vain too?"

"In vain…? Oh, I'm sorry if my language offended you. Anyway, yes, I do know how to cook, and I will, if—"

"Well, damn, you are a catch, aren't you?"

She dropped him on the silent, deserted street in front of the Holiday Inn. She didn't want to see him ever again, and she didn't have much faith that she would see her five hundred dollars again either. She fully intended to take it out of her roommate's Tupperware earnings.

Chapter Two

The apartment building on Ocean View was much different from what Reid was used to back home. A small swimming pool was encircled by an ironwork fence in front of a two-story stucco building with an outside staircase. The lower floor was painted white and the upper a sort of Pepto-Bismol pink. The overall impression suggested a cheap motel in an isolated desert town. There were only eight apartments, four up and four down. The building wasn't very secure or very private, but it was new and clean.

In spite of the name of the street, it had no view of the ocean. So far he had only seen the Pacific, sparkling under a clear blue sky, when he had flown back to Chicago, later than he had planned because of his court appearance, to box up what he wanted to ship here and hand his condo key over to his friend Noah. It had been twenty degrees and snowing in Chicago. Here the sun was too warm for an overcoat, but any whiff of sea air was blocked by the reek of chlorine from the pool.

He carried two shopping bags up the flight of concrete steps, found the apartment number on a brass plate on the door, and rang the matching doorbell. Jane had been cheerful but vague on the phone, and he wasn't sure of his welcome. He didn't remember exactly what she looked like but was reasonably confident it was she who opened the door—unnaturally red hair, a small, beaded ring in one nostril, large hoops dangling from her ears, a skimpy green tank top, tight jean shorts, and bare feet.

She smiled tentatively. "Yes?"

"Hi," he said. "Reid Lucas? We spoke on the phone?"

"Oh, yeah." She still sounded vague. She glanced at the shopping bags. "What's all this?"

"I didn't know what you would have—you know, utensils, spices—so I brought everything."

"Oh, okay. Come in if you're going to." She unlatched the screen door and wandered off.

Reid carried his bags inside and closed the door. She was out of sight, and he surveyed the living room. It was bigger than he would have expected from the exterior, carpeted in soft beige, the furniture sturdy if a little bland. The most personal touches were the framed photographs on the wooden mantel above the electric fireplace. He took a step closer out of curiosity. One picture was of Jane in a white cap and gown, a few years younger but with the same red hair and piercing. The other was of her roommate Alyssa and an older man with his arm draped across her shoulders. He wore a familiar uniform—CCPD. Her father was a cop? That was how she knew the DUI fine and the bail for a first offense?

Jane appeared in a doorway and beckoned, and he followed her into a galley-style eat-in kitchen. It was nearly all white, but the mosaic tile backsplash was a nice touch. "Whatcha gonna cook?" she asked. She perched on the counter and smiled at him.

"Something good," he said. He glanced around. There was a good gas range and generous workspace.

He lifted one shopping bag to the countertop next to her and started taking things out.

She peered into the bag. "Fancy schmancy," she said.

Was she going to watch and kibitz the whole time? He reminded himself this was an obligation, a penance even, not a pleasure outing, although he always enjoyed cooking. "Where's your roommate?" he asked. Jane had said her shift ended at four. He didn't feel entitled to use Alyssa's name yet.

"Church," she said succinctly and circled her temple with one finger in the universal sign for crazy.

He filled a pot with water and set it to boil. "I saw the picture in the other room. Her father is a police officer?"

"So is she."

He almost dropped the skillet. "Oh, my God!"

Jane was amused. "She didn't tell you that, huh? When you got her out of bed to bail you out?"

"No," he said. "If your cell phone hadn't been turned off, would you have come?"

"If I wasn't too busy—if you know what I mean. I'd a made you buy some Tupperware, of course. Whoa, that's a sharp knife."

"I won't stab anybody," he promised.

"You're funny," she said. "*And* you can cook. Why aren't you married?"

He kept his tone light but told her the truth. "I have a bad habit of falling in love with married women."

"And none of them would get a divorce and grab you?" she asked. "Well, you're in luck. Alyssa is married."

He kept his cool. "If she's married, why does she

live here with you?"

Jane swung her legs. "I'm nicer than her husband," she said. She had a girlish voice, but she was wearing the same seductively adult perfume he remembered from their first meeting.

"I'm sure you are."

"Can I help?" she asked.

"You could set the table," he suggested.

She nodded toward the grater. "You know you can buy grated cheese?"

"I did not know that," he said. "What will they think of next?"

"You *are* funny." She slid off the counter, stretched and yawned, and then opened a cupboard and took out plates. Reid began sautéing the onion and green pepper, filling the kitchen with pungent odors. "It smells good already," Jane said.

"I like the smell of onions too," he said. He added the ground beef.

"Don't they make you cry when you chop them?"

"Not if you know the trick," he said.

"Is it a secret?"

"Oh, I have lots of secrets," he assured her. "So…what do you do besides sell Tupperware? *You're* not a cop, are you?"

"Fat chance. I drive a school bus."

"I would not have guessed that."

"What do you do? You said you had a job interview?"

"Designing software. I just hope the boss doesn't expect me to drink with him again."

"Oh, yeah. How'd you do in court?"

"Fine and unsupervised probation, and I'll have to

take the bus to work for a month and everywhere else for four. Plus, I had to pay to have the rental car towed back to the agency and for the DUI program, and when I buy a car, I'll have to pay for an ignition interlock device."

"Ouch," she said cheerfully. "You schlepped all this here on the bus?"

"I did." He briskly chopped celery with the sharpest knife.

"Celery?" She helped herself to a small chunk.

"It's the secret ingredient," he said. "Don't tell." He emptied the contents of the cutting board into the skillet and picked up a can of tomatoes. "Oh—I hope you have a can opener."

"Yep." She opened a drawer and handed him one, the kind that could be set on top of the can to open it automatically.

"Nice," he said.

"This is fun," she said. "I like cooking with you. We never cook." They heard the door close in the living room, and she added, "Alyssa's home."

Reid felt himself getting tense for no reason. His obligation to her loomed large, of course, and he barely knew her. Still, she wasn't going to arrest him if she didn't like the pasta. He concentrated on stirring and adding tomatoes, mushrooms, and oregano, while hearing random sounds elsewhere in the house. He had just measured and slid the spaghetti into the boiling water when Alyssa came into the kitchen.

"Hi," Jane said. "We're cooking. This is—" She had forgotten his name.

"Reid Lucas," he said quickly.

"I know who he is," Alyssa said.

He couldn't help staring at her. She was prettier than he had remembered, even with her long, dark hair done up in a tight bun and wearing almost no makeup and an intimidating navy blue uniform. He was glad Jane had warned him about that. At least she wasn't wearing a gun or badge, and he had never seen a CCPD officer in a hat. There was nothing unfeminine about her face with its big dark eyes and curving lips.

"His real name is Emerson," she said. Her voice was different than he had remembered, too, softer, even though she still sounded a little annoyed with him.

"Emerson?" Jane repeated, incredulous.

"He can't help his name," Alyssa said. The meat was browning nicely, and Reid kept his gaze on it.

Jane was perched on the counter again, and Alyssa leaned on the wall by the table, keeping her distance. "He likes married women," Jane said, "but he swore when I told him you're a cop."

"He swears a lot."

"Sorry," Reid said. "I wasn't at my best the other night. But the biblical prohibition against taking God's name in vain was more to do with using it in magical incantations."

A brief, surprised silence followed. "I thought you didn't believe in God," Alyssa said.

"I didn't say that. I think religion is a private matter. Anyway, I *have* studied the Bible."

"Why?" she asked.

He looked up at her. "Because it's interesting," he said. She was regarding him with more attention than before. He didn't think she knew how pretty she was. As usual, he was attracted to the wrong one. If he wanted to get laid—which he didn't—Jane would be much easier. Aside from the nose piercing and bright hair, she was attractive enough—cute, anyway—and fun, outgoing, unconstrained. Maybe he was drawn to Alyssa because she had appeared to him as an angel of mercy in the police station. Or maybe, as his friend Noah had suggested, he was afraid of commitment and therefore attracted to the unattainable. To distract himself from her eyes, he drained the pasta.

"I don't think it's done yet," she objected.

"It's not," he agreed. He greased the baking dish, carefully layered half of the spaghetti, meat mixture, and Cheddar cheese into it, and then added a second layer of each.

Jane watched intently as he thoroughly mixed the mushroom soup with water and poured it over the entire dish. "He *is* good at this," she commented.

"Thank you," he said.

"I mean, you know, for a software designer. He's a computer geek," she explained to Alyssa. He picked up the Parmesan cheese, and Jane handed him the grater like a surgical nurse passing a scalpel. "I mean, doesn't he look like a computer geek?" He sprinkled grated cheese on top, giving the dish its finishing touch.

"He looks like a drunk driver," Alyssa said, but he didn't have to see her face to tell she had meant it as a joke. He ignored them and slid the baking dish into the oven. As always, he savored the warmth of a kitchen in full cooking mode. It was one of his favorite things.

"Now what?" Jane asked.

"The salad," he said and opened the second shopping bag.

"Jane, could I see you for a minute in the other room?" Alyssa said. It wasn't a question, and she left the kitchen at once.

Jane didn't hurry after her. "Keep up the good work," she said. "We'll be right back."

He started the salad, glad of the chance to do so without an audience. He could hear the murmur of voices in the living room and wondered what they were talking about. He wouldn't eavesdrop, but he hoped for a clue.

Given time to catch his breath, he reviewed the situation and felt mostly puzzlement. The two women did not seem like an obvious pairing as roommates or friends, and his reaction to Alyssa was misplaced, mistimed, and unnerving. It wasn't just that she was pretty or had rescued him. In her presence he felt as he had the entire time in the police station—stunned.

After a few minutes, the voices came closer, and then Jane sauntered in alone.

****

Alyssa frowned at herself in the mirror over her dresser. What was this guy up to? She had made sure it was only DUI he was arrested for before she bailed him out. Okay, that stuff happened. It wasn't as if good people couldn't be arrested, but something disturbing here made her suspicious. The helpless puppy dog act on the phone and at the police station—"Please…I'm so sorry"—and now he was here in their kitchen, making himself at home and cooking dinner. He had not been evasive, except about meeting Jane, but her police instincts told her he was hiding something. Jane didn't do background checks on her pickups, after all. He could have a criminal record somewhere else.

He had wanted access to them or their apartment enough to cook an entire meal to gain entrée. Was he a con man, a burglar, a rapist? Had he sworn when he found out she was a police officer because he knew she wouldn't be an easy victim or let her roommate be one? He didn't have the slick approach of a salesman, but some scams were based on eliciting sympathy from the mark.

Maybe it wasn't a con or an act. Maybe he was as harmless as he seemed and wanted to get in good with them so he could take advantage of their friendship. His approach was original, anyway. The way into a woman's apartment is through her kitchen? Jane had been watching him cook, but they would be wise to make sure he partook himself before assuming the food wasn't drugged or poisoned.

Then again, maybe she had been on the job too long and was just paranoid. She finished brushing her hair and opened a drawer to get a sweater. The one she chose was warm and comfortable. That it was also pretty was not a consideration.

****

Alyssa didn't come back until the salad was finished and the garlic bread in the broiler. Enticing smells filled the kitchen, and her scent, subtler than Jane's, added to the mix. She had undone her hair and changed from her uniform into blue jeans and a pink turtleneck sweater.

"Jane said you were at church?" he asked before she could say anything. "I noticed a beautiful one at the end of the street."

"Yes. The Greek Orthodox church. It is pretty, but I went to St. Anthony's."

"And you wear your uniform to church?"

"Sometimes. And no, I didn't take my gun inside."

Silence followed, and he tried again. "How did you two meet?"

"She arrested me," Jane confessed.

"You're joking."

"No, she did."

"You give new meaning to the phrase *partners in crime*. For what?"

"Practicing my constitutional right to free speech."

"Violating a city ordinance," Alyssa corrected.

"I forgave her," Jane said. "It wasn't her call."

"You broke the law."

"I'm glad I'm not the only one," Reid commented.

"Shall we forgive him?" Jane asked Alyssa.

"Maybe," she said, leaning back against the wall. "Did you bring a bottle of wine?"

"No, but I have your check." He pulled out his wallet and retrieved it. "I didn't think wine would be wise, when you already think I'm a drunk."

"DUIs do give that impression." She glanced at the check and passed it to Jane.

"I only had one drink."

"More likely three. The arresting officer said you were unsteady, and you were talking too loud when I picked you up. If you only had one drink, you must have an extremely low tolerance."

"Or it was a very strong drink," Jane said. She looked at the check. "Oh, Reid is your middle name. Not like an alias. R-E-I-D," she added to Alyssa. "Emerson Reid Lucas—sounds like a law firm." She was still studying the check. "Chicago? Is that where you're from?"

"Yes."

"Whoa! Cold back there this time of year."

"Yeah," he agreed. "I don't know how you people even know what season it is."

Alyssa made a rude sound.

"Is she always like this, or is it me?" he asked Jane.

"She's had a hard week."

He glanced at the table, which was set for three. "You know, I don't have to stay. I'm only here to cook."

"We won't bite," Alyssa said.

"She's had her rabies shots," Jane offered. "Anyway, we know it's October when the Christmas lights go up." She grinned.

The oven timer dinged, and for a while they were all busy getting everything on the table. Alyssa politely asked Reid what he wanted to drink.

"Ice water would be fine," he said.

She poured it without comment and got Cokes for herself and her roommate. As soon as they were all seated, she asked, "Why Carroll City? Long way from Chicago."

"The way things are these days," he said, "you go where the job is."

"Designing software? So what is that like? You sit at a computer all day?"

"A lot of it is," he admitted. "But I expect to do some field work to find out what the client needs. Software is not just on the screen. It has to work in the real world."

She looked at him, curious now. "How so?"

"For example, suppose you want your computer to turn on the lights when you come home or adjust the thermostat—"

"Yeah, okay."

Jane smiled as she finished a mouthful of spaghetti. "This is really good, Reid."

Her roommate was more cautious. "I didn't think it would be good baked, but it's not bad."

"I think she likes it," Jane said.

"The spices," Alyssa said vaguely and added apologetically, "Men who cook are rare in my experience, so…"

"All the great chefs are men," he pointed out.

"Julia Child," Jane put in.

"But you aren't a chef," Alyssa said. "You design software. Like what kind? For what? To turn on the lights?" She wasn't offering a challenge, only curiosity. She gazed at him intently as she took another bite.

"Yeah, so he can pay his electric bill," Jane said.

"My first project is an automated system for a chemical company," Reid said. "And yes, to pay my electric bill, when I have one. I've been apartment hunting on the bus. I'm still in the motel with just a microwave, so the kitchen here was a treat."

"Where did you learn to cook?" Jane asked.

"My mother was a great cook," he said. "And I picked things up along the way." To deflect more questions, he asked one of his own. "How long have you been a police officer?"

"Five years."

"Because your dad was on the force?"

"How did you know?"

"The picture in the living room," he said. "It must be a very challenging job."

"Sometimes," she said,

"And you had a bad week?"

"I guess you did too." Her tone had become more

sympathetic.

Reid smiled at Jane. "How about you? How was your week?"

"It was okay. The little monsters are quieter than they used to be, y'know? They all have their noses in their iPads and shit."

"Bunch of zombies," Alyssa agreed. "What's in this salad dressing?"

"Olive oil, lemon juice, salt, and garlic."

"Nice," Jane said approvingly. "Is this radicchio? Wanta cook for us every night?"

He took it as a joke and laughed appreciatively. It wasn't his best salad. Maybe it needed more fennel. Maybe Alyssa unnerved him.

"No, we would get fat," she said. She was enjoying the food and had brightened a little. She pointed her fork at Reid. "Okay, now I want to hear the long story about how you two met."

Jane giggled. "It's not that long."

"Let me guess. In a bar. Who picked up who?"

"In an elevator," Jane corrected. "There was this guy."

"Big ugly guy," Reid said. He gestured to indicate his size.

"Actually, he was kind of cute. Wavy hair, broad shoulders, and wow, he was dressed really sharp. Gorgeous tie anyway, expensive suit, nice shoes. I think they were Tanino Crisci."

Alyssa rolled her eyes.

"Don't scoff," Jane said. "They're like over a thousand dollars a pair."

"For *shoes*?" Reid was appalled.

"They were probably knockoffs," Alyssa

suggested.

"She thinks everybody's a phony," Jane said. "She's been a cop too long. Anyway, this guy was pretty impressive, except he knew it, and that is the biggest turn-off. And jeez, Reid, did you see his fingernails? Bet that was an expensive manicure."

"I didn't notice his fingernails," he admitted, "but I did notice where he put his hands."

"Hand," she corrected. "He was carrying a briefcase. Real leather. He had on leather gloves, too, but he took one off—with his teeth, which is kind of low class—before he touched me. Anyway, he puts his hand on me and asks, like, 'How much?' "

"Maybe if you wouldn't dress like a hooker..." Alyssa said.

"My dress almost covered my knees," Jane protested. "And this guy I never seen before," she continued, gesturing toward Reid, "like yanks the guy's hand off me and says—I forget, what did you say?"

"You've made a mistake, something like that."

"So, the suit got off, and I asked Reid if he wanted to buy me a drink."

"And I said she had the wrong idea about me."

She giggled. "No, he said he had an interview, but he was real polite about it, so I gave him my card, and we talked about Tupperware and stuff." A thought struck her. "It would have been awkward if the suit had been your interviewer."

Reid shook his head. "No, he was a young guy in jeans, an internet startup type. I'd guess twenty-two. It's a little scary having such a young kid as a boss, but he seems okay so far."

"Aside from getting you drunk," Alyssa said.

"I had one drink!"

"Give him a break, Liss," Jane said. "He cooked us this great meal."

Alyssa gave him a forgiving smile. He was glad to know she *could* smile. "Sorry," she said. "Tell us about Chicago."

Talking about his hometown was easy enough and took them through a good part of the meal. He kept his description general, the kinds of things tourists would comment on—the high-rises that dwarfed Carroll City's tallest buildings, the vintage brownstones, Lake Michigan, the Brookfield Zoo, the Miracle Mile, Millennium Park, green dye in the Chicago River on St. Patrick's Day. At one point, Jane interjected, "You don't sound like you're from Chicago."

"You mean he doesn't have a stereotypical accent," Alyssa clarified. "Cubs or White Sox?" she asked.

"Officially both, but…Cubs."

"Good for you."

Nothing had been said about anybody's marital status, but the tone had become friendlier, and he was bold enough to say, "Jane said you're married?"

She made a dismissive gesture but didn't seem annoyed. "Technically. He's seriously Catholic, so no divorce, but he's trying to get a church annulment."

"Which can take *years*," Jane said. "No religion can be worth that."

"How would you know?" Alyssa asked. "Anyway, the process is supposed to be faster now, since Pope Francis." He wanted to ask if she was seriously Catholic too but reminded himself of his own tenet— faith was a private matter. He had a hard enough time knowing what to believe without trying to explain it.

They were treating him in a casual, friendly way now, and let him help clear the table and load the dishwasher. He washed the utensils he had brought with him in the sink. "Whereabouts are you apartment hunting?" Alyssa asked.

"Close to work," he said. "It has to be on a bus line for now. I'll find somewhere more permanent later when I can buy a car."

"You should get a roommate," Jane said. "It's a blast."

"Room with the startup kid," Alyssa suggested. "That should be fun. You can get drunk every night."

"Okay," he said. He was tired of the joke, but she had gotten out of bed to bail him out—maybe she was entitled. "I'll leave the rest of the cheese," he told Jane. "If you reheat the leftovers, you can add a little cheese, but use the oven, not the microwave. It takes a little more time, but it stays hot longer."

"Why?" she asked with the perfect curiosity of a child.

"Don't encourage her," Alyssa advised. "She's like a two-year-old. You work downtown? You might try the Crown Ridge neighborhood. It's not far away and mostly mid-century modern apartment buildings. You can walk to restaurants and grocery stores, too."

"Thanks," he said. "I haven't seen much of that here."

"It's not Chicago, but people are pretty friendly."

"I've noticed," he said. Would he have called Jane to bail him out in Chicago?

When he was finished washing up, he packed everything and got ready to leave.

"Don't rush off," Alyssa said, but she was merely

being polite.

"My job here is done," he said. "Thanks for the use of your kitchen and for your hospitality."

Alyssa glanced at the shopping bags and said, "I could give you a ride."

"Thanks, but then I'd owe you another meal." He didn't want to be further indebted to her, as much as he would like an excuse to see her again.

****

"That was seriously strange," Alyssa said when he was gone. "What do you think he was up to?"

"He was discharging his obligation to you," Jane reminded her. "Don't be paranoid. Anyway, he doesn't know anybody else in town except his dipso kid boss, and he's got to be lonely. I liked him."

It wasn't as if she didn't think he was likeable. Maybe Jane was right, and she had been a cop too long to take anyone at face value. But what kind of man talked his way into the apartment of two women and…cooked for them?

Chapter Three

Reid took the Sunday newspaper over near the window where the light was better and began the tedious business of marking possible apartment rentals. As he refolded the classified listings, he happened to see an item on the front of the Local section. The weekly summary of the news included the developments in the Warren trial. What had caught his eye was a name—*Officer Alyssa Knight, daughter of retired Police Captain Oliver Sharpe, underwent two days of exhaustive and confrontational cross-examination that did not alter her testimony.* This, no doubt, was her hard week. He was sure police officers didn't enjoy testifying in court even under the best circumstances.

He marked several locations on his city map and consulted the transit system website to plan the day's travels. He was getting used to taking the bus, and he could now read a paperback novel and manage not to miss his stop even when the narrative got exciting.

He began in Crown Ridge, because Alyssa had recommended it. The first thing he noticed was the volume of foot traffic. As she had promised, the neighborhood had plenty of restaurants and a grocery store, not to mention bookstores, a pharmacy, a bank, and a movie theater within walking distance of multi-level apartment buildings. They didn't soar skyward like the ones he was used to, but at least they resembled someplace he might want to live.

Next, he noticed an unusual number of same-sex pairs with linked hands among the pedestrians and a bar named after Harvey Milk. If there was such a thing as a gay neighborhood, this was one. After a few minutes, he amended the label to gay-friendly, because he saw lots of opposite-sex couples too.

He looked at several of the rentals he had marked. They were not what he wanted in a permanent residence, but they might do for now. What *did* he want? In short, Chicago. High rises with doormen and spectacular city views from tiny balconies, an intense urban vibe entirely missing here, even though Carroll City was a good-sized metropolis. The Crown Ridge neighborhood, if not the entire city, had a decidedly small-town feel.

He surprised himself by paying a deposit and signing a six-month lease for a one-bedroom apartment on the fifth floor of a six-floor building. A large green park dominated the view, and a glimpse of the bay promised spectacular sunsets. It had as much space as he needed and a better kitchen than Jane and Alyssa's—stainless steel appliances, granite countertops, double oven, gas range, and a roomy pantry. Not to mention hardwood floors and plenty of windows throughout, an unexpectedly wide balcony, a big bathroom with a tiled shower, a stacked washer and dryer, a large bedroom complete with king-sized bed, and a flat screen TV in the comfortable living room. He would have an assigned space in the attached garage when he had a car to park there, and meanwhile he would be right on the number twelve bus route. A branch library was only two blocks away.

****

Reid arrived at Conavard Software a little early on Monday morning, but several people were ahead of him and busy on their phones or computers. He headed to the office he had begun to think of as his own and found Baird's door closed, as it never was when he was in. Okay, points for arriving ahead of the boss.

His own office was tiny, but had a large window, a decent-sized desk, and an ergonomic chair. He hadn't been working here long enough for it to be cluttered, but he did have a favorite coffee mug and a page-a-day calendar beside his computer. He left the door open because most of the others did. He was deep into trying to understand enough about polymers to communicate effectively with Velazquez Chemical, when Randy Goff came to lounge in his doorway.

Goff was tall and rangy, in his late thirties, and annoyingly cynical. "Hey, uh—" Goff had forgotten his name and was on the brink of saying something like "new guy," but he let it go and asked, "What's with Baird?"

"Not in yet, I guess."

"No, his car's in the garage."

Reid shrugged. He was not his supervisor's keeper.

Goff shrugged too and sauntered on toward the men's room. Reid turned back to his computer, and ten seconds later Goff said, "Oh, shit," very loudly and then, even louder, "*Holy shit!*"

A couple of other engineers hurried past his door, and Reid got up and went out in the hall to see what was going on. Goff emerged from the men's room, his face oddly pale, and said, "Call 911." While Reid hesitated, the other two were already on their phones as they hurried into the men's room to see for themselves. He followed more slowly.

The first thing he saw, as he stared past the others, was a black shoe. Reluctantly he stepped farther inside. Baird's wire-rim glasses lay on the floor beside his inert form, twisted out of shape and speckled with brown spots. A large reddish-brown stain spread around the short spiky blondish hair. His face was whiter than Goff's had been, and his eyes were open, staring, and blank.

Goff was in a stall, throwing up.

****

Alyssa stood beside her patrol car, having just explained to a concerned citizen that the gun-toting evildoer she had reported was only a college professor with a furled black umbrella. She and her partner, Ty Hendrix, were laughing about the woman's reaction when the call came in. "Knight, you're wanted downtown."

"Why?" she asked as she got into the car to comply.

"Suspect in Homicide says you're his alibi."

"Not unless I gave him a ticket," she said. She didn't have a clue what this was about.

Traffic was light, and they were at headquarters in minutes. She took the elevator up and strode into Homicide. She was frankly envious of the detectives here, with their big desks and bigger salaries and interesting and important cases. One of them glanced at her and pointed to an interview room.

She recognized him through the glass before she opened the door—Emerson Reid Lucas. "Now what did you do?" she asked.

He didn't say anything, but she could tell he was glad to see her.

"You know this guy?" Detective Macias asked.

"Slightly," Alyssa said. "What's this about?"

"He claims he spent Saturday evening with you."

"Part of it. My roommate and me. He's her friend."

"What part?" Macias asked. He picked up a pen.

"He was there when I got home about five and left—sevenish?" She looked to Reid for agreement. "My roommate can confirm. What's this about?" she repeated. "He's been in town like a week and he's murdering people?"

Detective Macias rose, led her out of the interview room, and closed the door before he said anything. "His boss is dead. I kind of like him for it. He's the newest employee and has a recent DUI, plus his name came up in a homicide in Chicago."

"He was a suspect?" Alyssa was deeply surprised. Whatever else he was up to, she wouldn't have imagined him a killer. Was this the real reason he had left Chicago?

"Person of interest."

"So you think he's a serial killer? Jeez, look at him."

"I did. That's exactly what serial killers look like. Human beings are by definition capable of murder. Trust me. Most of the time it's the quiet ones."

"Time of death?" she asked.

"M.E. thinks Saturday night, probably eight to midnight."

"So, I didn't help much," she said. Had this been the point of cooking dinner for them? To establish an alibi?

"It's a start," Macias said. He asked for Jane's name and number and wrote them in his notebook.

"Why would he kill his boss? You don't come halfway across the country to take a job and kill your meal ticket."

Macias shrugged.

"Is he under arrest?"

"Not yet."

"Good. I'm not bailing him out again." The detective raised his eyebrows, and to derail a dangerous line of questioning, she asked, "Who else are you talking to?"

"The other employees—and the wife, of course."

"He's married? Lucas said he was just a kid."

"Twenty-seven. He did look younger, but yeah, definitely married. She's a looker, too. Dunno what a piece like that sees in these nerdy types."

"Piece?" Alyssa repeated.

"Oh, sorry," he said unrepentantly. "Lady. The grieving widow." He rolled his eyes.

"Go easy on Lucas," she suggested. "He didn't skip out on the Chicago case, did he?" Surely, if he was a fugitive, he wouldn't have used his own name.

"No, and apparently the husband did it, but it does raise questions when the same person is on the periphery of two murders in a short time. I don't believe in coincidences."

She didn't either, but she said, "They do happen, though," defending him when he might not deserve it. She kept thinking of him in her kitchen, intent on cooking a meal for her and Jane, to pay her back for bailing him out. He was a stranger to her, still a stranger.

"He say anything else to you about the deceased? Besides how young he was?"

"Only that he took him out for a drink after the interview—which led to the DUI. Who kills his boss for getting him drunk?"

Macias shrugged.

"Did he tell you he took public transit? He may not know you can find out where his bus pass was used." He couldn't prove who had used it, but it was a start, and a driver or passenger might remember him.

"We're on it," Macias said. He waved a hand at her and ambled back into the interview room. Through the window she saw Reid look up as he entered but couldn't read his expression. Not my problem, she thought, and headed back to work.

****

Baird's funeral—or memorial service, as his body had not been released by the police for burial—was held at St. Dunstan's Episcopal Church. Reid attended only because it was expected. Everyone else at Conavard was going. He didn't know anyone well enough to ask for a lift, and taking the bus proved inconvenient, so he took a taxi.

The church was dimly lit and had a faint odor of incense. About thirty people were present, of whom Reid recognized only his co-workers. A few of them nodded hello, but for the most part he was ignored.

He had known he would hear what a wonderful person Baird was and how joyful his return to his Creator would be, but the main thrust of the rector's message hit closer to home. "There is enough grief in the world to cause us all to sink into despair. The only

31

path through such despair is through God, who forgives us our sins, and through our own forgiveness of others. St. Paul tells us all have sinned and come short of the glory of God. We are all sinners, and we can all be forgiven. We must forgive those who injure us—yes, even those who do the greatest violence to us and to those we love—and we must forgive ourselves for falling short, through our sins, of the glory God offers us."

Chapter Four

Reid's guests, the first he had had, arrived while he was putting the salad in the refrigerator to chill. Jane was the one who had called to see if he was all right. She was a good-hearted girl. He had told her about his new apartment, and she wanted to see it. She didn't ask if he had killed Baird. Before he had time to think about it, he had invited her to dinner. Neither of them had mentioned Alyssa's name, but after she hung up, he'd realized she had said "we" twice.

He opened the door with an anticipatory thrill that he knew was out of place. Jane came in first and gave him a quick kiss on the cheek. She wore a sleeveless white blouse, and her tan skirt ended inches above her knees. She had no sweater, and it was cold outside—cold by Southern California standards anyway, at least twenty degrees warmer than Chicago. It had been sunny most of the day, but clouds had begun to form now, with rain in the forecast.

"Why do I always see you in kitchens and police stations?" Alyssa asked, coming in behind Jane. She was out of uniform in black slacks and a long-sleeved blouse with diagonal squares of pastel colors. Her hair was tied back in a ponytail instead of the more severe bun.

"I'm sorry. I didn't know they would make you come downtown."

"At least they didn't wake me up." She said it without any sting in the words; she was only teasing. She held up the short coat she had shed at the door. Reid pointed to the closet outside the kitchen, and she opened the door to hang it up. "Interesting," she said, eyeing the interior, which contained nothing except empty hangers. He still had not much more than he had carried from Chicago in his suitcase, except in the kitchen, where he had installed most of what he had shipped.

"Thanks for the tip about Crown Ridge," he said. "I like it here."

"I knew you would," she said. "It's a great neighborhood. I was always glad to be assigned to this precinct."

"What are you cooking for us?" Jane asked. "It smells great."

"Lamb," he said. "I hope that's okay." He had marinated it overnight in rosemary, honey, mustard, ground pepper, and lemon zest, so he hadn't had to do much this evening. It had filled the apartment with a rich, musky aroma, and the kitchen was comfortably warm, two things he associated with his childhood, with home.

"It doesn't bother you to cook an innocent little baby lamb?" Alyssa asked.

"No…serial killer that I am." They didn't laugh at his macabre joke. "Does it bother you to eat it?"

"Not me," Jane said. "Not when it smells so good."

"I've only had lamb once," Alyssa said. "It was delicious, very tender."

"I finished the salad, and the lamb will be in the oven for a while, so I should show you the apartment while we're waiting."

Jane nodded eagerly. Alyssa said nothing but followed them down the hall. They admired the balcony and the bathroom in particular. Jane exclaimed over the tile in the shower, but cautioned him, "You can't take long showers, you know. We have water restrictions in Southern California."

"Can you afford all this?" Alyssa asked. "Aren't you out of a job?"

"Not so far," he said. "Most of the clients have stayed, and you know what they say, any publicity is good publicity."

"So, who's the boss?"

"Mrs. Baird is now the owner. The associate who's been at Conavard the longest is temporarily in charge. Everything is still up in the air, but I'm concentrating on my own projects right now."

"What do you think of Mrs. Baird?" Alyssa asked with studied indifference.

"Frankly? She's scary. She doesn't know anything about software or business, and she…"

"Do you think she killed her husband?"

He didn't give her a quick answer. He considered the question while they stood in the bedroom doorway and Jane checked out the view from the large window. He was a little distracted by Alyssa's nearness. "No," he said finally.

"She's always thinking like a cop," Jane said apologetically.

Try as he might, he couldn't think of a thing to say in response.

"Hey!" she said. "Did you see that?"

"What?" Reid and Alyssa asked in unison, and a

second later they heard a low growl of thunder.

"Lightning," Jane said unnecessarily. They all saw the next flash, which lit up the bedroom, followed immediately by a crash that shook the building. The lights blinked off. "Oops," she said. Large drops of rain splattered against the bedroom window.

Reid turned to Alyssa. "This happen a lot?" he asked. He had been led to believe Carroll City's weather could be summed up in one word—boring.

"No. Hardly ever."

"Climate change," Jane said sagely. She joined them in the hall, and they waited for another flash or rumble or for the lights to come back on. "Oh, the lamb!" she said.

"The oven is gas," Reid assured her. "It will be fine. The timer, though…" He glanced at his watch, trying to remember when he had put the roast in the oven. They followed him into the kitchen. The light from the windows kept it from being too dark inside, but it was eerily dim. He reached automatically for a light switch, which made him feel foolish, but at least Alyssa didn't notice.

"I don't suppose you have any candles," she said. "Or a hurricane lamp, anything like that. A flashlight?"

"Of course not. Oh—" He hurried back to the bathroom, where the night light plugged in above the sink doubled as an emergency light when the power was off. The property manager had pointed it out when he showed him the apartment. He took it back to the kitchen and set it in the middle of the table.

"Not exactly candlelight," he said, "but it will have to do."

"Do you have a landline?" Alyssa asked.

"Yes, in the living room." She left, and Reid raised his eyebrows at Jane questioningly.

She opened the door of the refrigerator, dark and quiet now, and took out the salad. "Oh, she's going to call CCG&E. There's like a recording? They know from your phone number where you are and if they have an outage in your area and how long it will take to fix."

"They couldn't know so soon."

"No," she agreed. She sampled the green pepper. "But they'll guess, usually wrong." She sounded very cheerful about the prospect.

"Put that back," he said. "I want it chilled."

"Plates?" she asked, glancing around.

"You're a guest," he told her. "Sit." He opened the oven door and checked the meat thermometer. "Close enough," he said, pulled on oven mitts, and lifted the roasting pan out.

She didn't sit and edged closer to watch as he peeled back the foil to reveal the nicely browned leg of lamb. "Scrumptious," she said.

"Sit," Reid said again. He set the table with his newly purchased dinnerware. He had four place settings—good thing he didn't have a lot of friends here. Jane was still standing, but she didn't get in the way.

Alyssa breezed in. She pointed to the light on the table and said, "That won't last forever, you know. The electricity will probably be out for several hours. There's never a dull moment with you, is there? DUI, murder, power outage…"

"I'm not responsible for the weather," he protested. He sliced the lamb and arranged it on his only platter and took the salad out of the refrigerator.

Jane gazed at the meat in admiration. "He really can cook, can't he?"

"Very impressive," Alyssa said dryly.

Jane reached for a piece of cucumber, and Reid feigned a slap at her hand. She grinned at him. "D'ja make dessert this time?" she asked.

"Cranberry pie," he said.

"I don't care much for pie," Alyssa said and added, in a less critical tone, "I never heard of cranberry pie."

"It sounds yummy," Jane said.

"What's your favorite dessert?" he asked Alyssa. He was idly curious—he didn't presume a future opportunity to please her.

"Chocolate cake," she said without hesitation.

"Of course," he said. "There's a reason why women crave chocolate, you know."

"He's kind of a know-it-all," Jane commented.

Reid ignored her. "What would you like to drink?" he asked. "I have pop—I think you call it 'soda' here—skim milk, ice water—except the icemaker won't work with the power off."

"Soda," both women said.

"No beer?" Alyssa asked.

"I don't think it's a good idea while I'm going to mandatory DUI classes."

"Wise decision," she said. "It's the next thing to AA." He poured sodas for all three of them and gestured for the ladies to sit.

The emergency light shed a cozy glow on the table, not as romantic as candlelight, but somehow conducive to a friendly intimacy. The sodas got a little warm without ice, but the lamb was perfect, tender and juicy.

"You eat like this all the time?" Jane asked.

"Cooking for one isn't much fun. Sometimes I make a sandwich or order pizza," he confessed, and they both admitted to a weakness for pepperoni.

They chatted about random things at first, and then Alyssa asked if he had family in Chicago.

"My father. My mother died two years ago."

"How sad," Jane said. "What's your father like?"

"Nice," he said. In the confiding atmosphere of the shared situation, he added, "A bit stodgy. He thinks my career will disappear when the computer fad ends."

"Yeah, I see that happening," Jane said, laughing. "My parents think I'm going to Hell. I'm a blot on the family escutcheon, whatever that is. No siblings?"

"I have a sister who lives in Texas. We aren't close."

"I have *lots* of sisters," Jane said and rolled her eyes.

"I know your dad is a cop," Reid said to Alyssa. "What about your mother?"

After a few seconds of strained silence, Jane jumped in with, "Not just any cop either. Real macho dude, big-shot captain, everybody's hero."

"A lot to live up to," he said, watching Alyssa, who kept her eyes on her plate.

"My mother has early-onset Alzheimer's," she said. "She doesn't always know me, but she still recognizes her favorite celebrities." She spoke with cool irony, but he could see how much it hurt.

He repressed an urge to touch her, comfort her. "Well, think about it," he said. "A face is all she knows about them. She doesn't know their personality quirks. She didn't diaper them and bandage their skinned knees. She has memories of your whole life, but a name and a face are all there is to celebrities, even when they pretend to be someone else. She doesn't know them with her heart."

Alyssa paused with her fork halfway to her mouth to stare at him.

"Maybe you're prettier than she remembers," he went on. "Do perps ever hit on you?"

She raised her eyebrows. "Perps?" She hadn't been very friendly, but she wasn't stuck up. She didn't know how beautiful she was, how appealing the little dent above her upper lip was, how her eyes changed color when she smiled. "Are *you* hitting on me?"

"Um…no." He wouldn't dare.

"You can be pretty sweet when you try. Why aren't you married?"

"Nobody I wanted to marry ever wanted to marry me," he said matter-of-factly.

"Who did you want to marry?" Jane asked. She helped herself to another slice of lamb and more salad and gave him a cheeky smile.

"My fifth-grade teacher," he said. "She was married. And so on. Why aren't *you* married?"

"I'm too young to die." She took a bite of lamb and smiled again.

"She didn't want to follow my bad example," Alyssa said.

He had meant to serve coffee with the cranberry pie, but it was a hit anyway. Jane only ate half of hers, but she obviously enjoyed it. She glanced at her watch and said, "I hate to eat and run, but I have a date."

"The elevator isn't working," Reid reminded her.

"Four flights of stairs," she said cheerfully. "That

should be fun." She turned to Alyssa and asked casually, "Do you want to go?" They had come in Jane's car.

"I'll get an Uber," Alyssa said, surprising Reid into silence.

He showed Jane to the door, and she thanked him prettily for dinner and kissed his cheek. "Be nice to Liss," she said. "She's not as tough as she pretends to be."

"I won't use my whip on her," he promised. "I'm going to have a real housewarming one of these days. Will you both come?"

"Are you going to cook?" she asked.

"Refreshments are usually served at a housewarming, yes."

"Good. We'll be here."

When he returned to the kitchen, Alyssa was eating pie, and she gave him a cool, appraising look. "So, who do you think killed the boss?" she asked.

He sat down and gave her his full attention. "This is why you stayed? To interrogate me?"

She shrugged.

"I don't know any of them well enough to guess," he said. "The police took all our fingerprints, so I guess they found some, and they haven't arrested anybody. I have no idea who it was."

"Somebody who had access to the building," she said.

"Maybe Jane did it," he suggested.

"Ha ha."

"Or the guy who hit on her, whoever he was."

"How do I know it wasn't you?" she asked.

"You were part of my alibi," he said.

"This isn't your first rodeo, is it? What happened in Chicago?"

"They told you about that?"

"Yep. I guess they had a good case against the husband…but you had an affair with her?"

Reid took a breath and made a choice to trust her. "No…I kissed her once. She laughed and pushed me away, but I think she was flattered. A few weeks later I tried again, and she didn't laugh. She held me off and said if I kissed her again, she would tell her husband. She didn't hold it against me, though. She was kind to me. She wasn't seductive or flirtatious, just friendly in a slightly distant way…and very kind. Forgiving."

"You never slept with her?" Alyssa asked, still skeptical.

"No. Not even close. But he thought we did."

"And he killed her." She paused and regarded him gravely. "And you blame yourself."

"Who *should* I blame?"

"The asshole who's in prison for it, for starters. He would have done it sooner or later anyway."

He shook his head. "Maybe, but…you know, survivor's guilt."

"Did you see a shrink?"

"I don't need some PhD to tell me it should have been me he went after. She didn't do anything."

"Was she the love of your life?" Her tone made light of the question.

"We'll never know."

"What was her name?" Did she plan to research the case?

"Sarah. She wasn't the first…unattainable woman I fell for."

"Your fifth-grade teacher. And…?"

"Another one left her husband for me and then decided she didn't want to be married to anyone. What about you? What happened with you and your husband?"

"I don't want to talk about it."

"Too painful?"

"Too embarrassing."

"Was he abusive?" He couldn't imagine a strong-minded woman like her tolerating anything of the sort for even a minute.

Alyssa hesitated, but he had told her his most painful truth. "Not physically," she said.

"Verbally?"

"Very passive aggressive, though, and so subtle I didn't even see it for a long time. It was interfering with my work. I spent a lot of time and energy rehearsing what I should say or what I should have said. One day I woke up and didn't want him to touch me ever again."

"His loss," Reid said.

"Meaning what?" she asked, ready to take offense.

He shrugged. "So, you're getting a divorce—or an annulment."

"On the grounds of fraud—that I never intended to enter into a valid marriage or have children."

"And did you?"

"Yes, but I wasn't planning to have a baby right away, and he didn't know I was on the pill. When he found out, I refused to stop."

"The nerve of these women—wanting to control their own bodies," Reid said in mock horror.

Alyssa gave him a look. "Anyway, we get along fine now. He hates me, and I loathe him, and we're great at being barely civil. Nice."

"And while you're waiting for the annulment, you can't marry anybody else."

"As if I'd want to."

He raised his eyebrows.

"What? Oh, I know what you think. You think I need a man," she said with a sneer.

"No, I don't."

"Yeah, well, maybe I do," she said, "but if I do, it's not you."

"I'm sure," he said as if it was of no consequence.

Alyssa looked a little miffed. "Too bad, though. Adultery would be easier. As grounds for annulment, I mean."

"But it would be a mortal sin," he pointed out.

"Maybe I'm losing my faith."

"I don't think so," he said. He didn't know her, but she had gone to church after work the day he had first cooked for her and Jane.

The lights flashed on, the refrigerator began to hum, and almost immediately the oven timer he had forgotten to turn off buzzed loudly. Reid got up to silence it and when he turned back to Alyssa the confiding vibe of the half-darkness was gone. "I'd better go," she said.

Chapter Five

Detective Macias politely ushered Reid into an interview room. He had answered everything he had been asked the first time and hadn't expected to be called back, but Macias acted as if it was commonplace. Maybe it was—detective work was probably tedious and repetitive, not like on TV. "Would you like a cup of coffee?" he asked.

Reid shook his head. He had had enough coffee today and didn't feel like wasting any time on these niceties.

Macias gestured to a chair and took one opposite. "Okay," he said. "I'll get right to the point. How well do you know Gloria Baird?"

"Mrs. Baird?" Not well enough to know her first name, for starters. "I don't know her at all. I've seen her…twice I think."

The detective studied him with weary patience. "Come on," he said. "Just between us."

"I don't know what you want. I don't know her."

"Easy on the eyes, isn't she?"

"I guess." He had found her a little obvious.

"I don't mind admitting I would love to hit that," Macias said. "I mean, really, did you get a load of her ass?"

Reid shifted uncomfortably in the hard wooden chair. "I don't…"

"Come on. You've got eyes. We're guys. We can't help noticing those things. The woman was born to be fucked. Am I right?" He raised his eyebrows, inviting agreement.

"I don't think this is appropriate," Reid said, but the feeble protest wasn't good enough. He should be irate, if not on Mrs. Baird's behalf, then on that of all women. This dude should be reported to Internal Affairs.

"Oh, you don't think it's *appropriate*?" Macias raised his eyebrows.

"She's the boss's wife. Widow. It's... disrespectful."

"You can do better than that. It makes you uncomfortable because you know I'm right, but you don't want to share. You want her all for yourself. Right?"

"Detective Macias, if you have questions about the case..."

"This is about the case," Macias said, and the ingratiating we're-just-guys tone was gone. "This is about motive. You were fucking Gloria Baird. Yes?"

"I don't even know her."

"No? How did you happen to take a job in Carroll City?"

"I needed a job. One was available here. I applied."

"You couldn't find one back home? I hear Chicago is having a tech boom these days."

Reid shrugged.

"Who told you about the job?"

"I found the listing on the internet."

"Sure about that? Gloria didn't tell you about it?" He made the name sound dirty—*Glow-ria.*

"I told you I didn't know her."

"So, you're trying to tell me it's a total coincidence that you work for the husband of a woman who lived in your hometown for fifteen years?"

"She was from Chicago?"

"You didn't know? She didn't mention it when you were introduced?"

"We weren't introduced. I saw her once with him, and she talked to the whole group after he died. Oh, and at the funeral of course."

"I think you're a liar, Mr. Lucas."

"I guess there's nothing I can do about that."

"You could try telling the truth. I don't believe in coincidences, and this is the second one involving you in this case. What are the odds?"

Reid shook his head. He didn't see the point of further protest. The guy was way off base, but nothing he could say was likely to change his mind. He thought of Alyssa and the games the police played on TV— good cop, bad cop. The detective was trying to get a rise out of him.

"We'll be following this up with the Chicago PD," Macias assured him. "We will find out the truth. Trust me. We know you had mutual acquaintances."

"Me and Mrs. Baird?" He didn't think so. Chicago was a big city. Macias was grasping at straws.

"Yeah, so let's skip the preliminaries and stipulate that you were fucking Mrs. Baird. Is that why you murdered her husband?"

Reid called his bluff. "What mutual acquaintances?" he asked. "Name one."

Macias glanced at his notebook. "Glenn D'Alessandro."

"I don't know who he is. I don't know what you're talking about."

"Oh, I think you do."

"No, I don't. And I have an alibi."

"A soft one. Somebody used your bus pass, but nobody remembers seeing you or any guy with two shopping bags."

Reid sat up straighter. "I didn't kill Baird," he said. "You're wasting your time if you want to find out who did. I'm not under arrest, so I don't need to be here."

Macias leaned back in his chair. "If you think knowing Captain Sharpe's kid is going to help you, forget it."

"You mean Officer Knight?" Reid asked coolly.

"Yes, Officer Knight. Everybody pretends otherwise, but she skates by on his reputation, which doesn't cut any ice with me. She's cute, though, huh?"

Reid stood up. "We're done here," he said.

"Oh, ho, did I touch a nerve?"

He didn't answer. He walked out and barely refrained from slamming the door.

****

The following Saturday, Jane showed up at his door, unexpected and certainly uninvited. She breezed in, dressed in another of her very short skirts, stiletto heels, and a low-cut, midriff-baring top. The outfit left nothing to the imagination. "Hi," she said. "What's cooking?" She laughed at her own joke.

"Nothing at the moment," he said.

"No? Wanna go out?"

"I wasn't expecting…"

"Surprise!" She bent one knee and slipped off one of her shoes. "Mind if I take these off? They're bloody uncomfortable."

"Why wear them, then?"

"Okay, thanks. Oh…you know, they're s'posed to make your legs sexier."

"I don't think you need any help," he said.

"Why, Emerson." She put her hand on his shoulder while she took off the other shoe and then kissed him on the cheek.

"The name is Reid," he said.

"I don't know—you look like an Emerson to me." He could have made a comment about her own name— she was no plain Jane—but he didn't. She apparently wasn't going anywhere, so he invited her to come in and have a seat. She waited for him to sit on the couch and sat right next to him. "So, you think I'm sexy?"

"You look good enough to eat," he said.

"Yeah?" She giggled and leaned forward to put a hand on his knee.

"But I'm not hungry right now."

"Oh." She removed her hand.

"Nothing personal."

"But you're not gay, right?"

"No."

"No, cuz I've seen the way you look at Alyssa."

"You're imagining things."

"No, I'm not."

"Why? Did she say something?"

"Nah. She's clueless."

"Why are you here, Jane?"

"I was bored. And hungry." She raised an eyebrow suggestively.

Reid sighed. "I'll see what I have in the kitchen," he said. "Turn on the TV if you want."

She grabbed the remote. "Got any good DVDs?"

He gestured toward the stack under the coffee table—he still hadn't squared everything away—and escaped into the kitchen. He checked the refrigerator, rejected a few possibilities, and found some pizza rolls in the freezer. He turned to the microwave, and Jane was standing at his elbow. "Jeez," he said.

"Oh, did I scare you?"

"Startled me," he amended. "I thought you were in the living room."

"I like to watch you cook," she said. "Are you going to put those in the microwave? You said the oven was better."

"It is, but—"

"What are they?"

"Hors d'oeuvres."

"No, that's like deviled eggs and canapés."

"Okay, they're appetizers. Double pepperoni."

"They'll stay hotter if you put them in the oven…you said."

"This is faster," he said, punching buttons. "I'm not your personal chef, you know."

Jane giggled. He steered her back into the living room. She popped a DVD in the player and sat back on the couch. "You like binge watching?" she asked.

"No. I don't watch much TV."

She drew him down beside her and stretched out on the couch with her bare feet in his lap. She had purple polish on her toenails and a small tattoo of a lock and key on one ankle.

"Jane…"

"What? You could at least give me a little foot rub."

"I don't think so." He took hold of her feet and put them on the floor where they belonged. She shrugged and sat up. She fast forwarded the DVD through ads and credits and turned the sound up a little too high to be comfortable. It was the first season of *Breaking Bad.* "I like Bryan Cranston," she said. "He seems like a good guy."

"Not in this."

"No, but he like supports children's causes and gay marriage and stuff. Good husband and father and like that."

"That's what you want in a man?" He didn't think she would find those qualities in bars.

"Eventually. But right now, y'know, a girl just wants to have fun. Don't you want to have fun, Emerson?"

"Reid. Right now, I mostly want to keep my job and stay out of jail."

"Those are good qualities in a man too. You should get a haircut, though."

The microwave dinged, and Reid went back to the kitchen to retrieve the pizza rolls and whip up an easy dipping sauce to accompany them. Mayo, honey, mustard, hot sauce…? He didn't know what to do about Jane. She was Alyssa's roommate, so he didn't want to offend her, but he was tired of her treating him like…what? What was his grievance against her? She was…she wasn't Alyssa. Did Alyssa think he needed a haircut too? He liked it a little long.

When he came back into the living room, Jane was stretched out again with her feet where he had been sitting. She looked settled and comfortable. He put the food on the coffee table and sat in the easy chair.

"Smells good," she said and reached lazily for a pizza roll. He sighed and took one too. It was a little tough, but the sauce helped. Jane didn't complain.

****

The housewarming was on a Saturday from four to seven. He kept it casual so people could drop by and stay as long as they wanted. Alyssa got off at four, and he didn't want it to be obvious she was the guest he most wanted to see. A young couple from the fourth floor, Tom and Ramona Halvorsen, were the first to arrive, followed by three of his co-workers. The pregnant wife was mainly interested in how his furniture compared to theirs, and the guys wanted to watch ESPN on the big-screen TV. He had made crab salad with lime and avocado—wonderfully abundant in southern California—and served it with crusty bread sticks, deviled eggs, and chilled bottles of Coke, Sprite, and iced tea. He was concerned that the guys might expect beer, but nobody said anything.

Jane and Alyssa arrived a little before five, both casually attractive in jeans. Jane's were low-slung, very tight, and topped by a blouse with a deep V-neck and tails tied to bare her midriff. Alyssa was the soul of modesty by comparison. Reid expected his coworkers to flock around the truly fetching Alyssa, but they only had eyes for Jane. Was being outshone by more obvious women the reason she believed she wasn't pretty?

"Don't tell anybody I'm a police officer," she instructed. "They'll get all weird." She then surprised him by getting into a discussion with Ramona Halvorsen about baby names.

****

At the end of February Reid received his restricted

driver's license. Since he was only allowed to drive to work and his DUI program, both of which were on a bus line, he took his time shopping for a new car. Alyssa and Jane made a few suggestions about good dealerships to try and on two memorable evenings accompanied him. No doubt they felt sorry for him and wanted to save him a few bus trips, but Jane at least enjoyed the hunt.

Alyssa he couldn't quite figure out. She was sometimes moody and distant, perhaps because of the stress of her job. Or maybe something more personal was troubling her? The interminable delay with the annulment? Or was it him? Maybe she was bored with Jane making a project of him? Or maybe her basic personality was always on the prickly side.

They were with him when he settled on a Chevy Malibu. He had been a little shocked by the prices, noticeably higher than the last time he had done this, but he could afford it. He didn't care about the color and would have taken whatever was available, but Jane favored red, and Alyssa thought he should get the blue one. He opted for blue, and Jane said smugly, "I knew it. He has conservative tastes."

"Anybody who'd buy a sedan these days," Alyssa agreed.

"You drive a sedan," he pointed out.

"I'm cheap." And yet she was not ungenerous— she had bailed out a stranger.

"She's like allergic to debt," Jane explained. "It's downright un-American."

"Why are you two friends? You're always criticizing each other."

"It's called teasing, doofus," Jane told him. She

nudged Alyssa. "I bet he gets his feelings hurt a lot."

"Not that I've noticed," she said. She surprised Reid with a smile that suggested something very like affection. He was dazzled but maintained his composure.

Jane drove the new car home for him, while Alyssa followed in Jane's SUV. Jane parked the Malibu in his designated spot, where it would spend most of the next few months. He planned to continue taking the bus to Conavard, but he would use the car when he had to go to a project site, which also counted as driving to work.

Chapter Six

Reid was both annoyed and concerned to be summoned to police headquarters again. He had a clear conscience, which didn't keep him from feeling a little uneasy as he was ushered into an interview room by a polite, poker-faced uniformed officer. He was left alone for about five minutes before Detective Macias charged in. He seemed annoyed too, slapped his steno-size notebook bulging with papers down on the table, and sat down with his arms crossed. "Mr. Lucas," he said.

"Detective Macias," Reid returned coolly.

"Do you know why you're here?"

"I assume something to do with Mr. Baird's murder."

"You're on unsupervised probation, but technically we could search your apartment without a warrant, so…"

"For a DUI?" He didn't think so.

Macias waved a hand dismissively. "I'm just saying save us both a lot of trouble. What would we find if we did search?"

"You mean like a murder weapon?"

Macias raised his eyebrows. "Why, do you have one?"

Reid didn't even bother to shake his head.

"No, we have the murder weapon," Macias continued. He nodded, acknowledging Reid's surprise.

"We're looking for the motive. If we search your apartment, are we going to find evidence of your...involvement with Mrs. Baird?" Same old question, but more formally worded—meaning what?

"I told you I don't even know the woman. Have you asked *her*?"

"She denies it, but I'm not just blowing smoke here. We have witnesses who heard Baird say he suspected she was cheating. Maybe it wasn't you, but I find it hard to believe she didn't have *anything* to do with it. Women like her...well, you know what I mean. So, can you help us figure out what the motive might have been? The motive tends to point the way to the perpetrator. Can you think of any reason...?"

"You're asking me why somebody would kill Baird? I barely knew him either. Robbery, maybe?"

"Nothing was taken except his wallet. The place was full of computers, and he was wearing an Omega watch worth thousands, and solid gold cufflinks. The killer didn't even take his cell phone. But I'm not asking you why somebody would want to kill your boss. I'm asking you why somebody would want to kill you."

****

Alyssa pulled in behind the gray BMW without recognizing it. Her mind was on what awaited her inside her parents' house, the well-kept two-story home she had grown up in. She got out of the car and had barely focused on the familiar vehicle when the front door of the house opened, and her husband came out. *Shit!* Two minutes slower getting started and she would have missed him.

He saw her at once and sauntered closer. "Well,

well," he said. "If it isn't Little Miss Super Cop." He looked her over in a way she didn't like, as if he wasn't sure she was worth his time.

"Hello, Paul," she said neutrally. "How are you?"

"Oh, is that supposed to make me think you care?"

"It's a standard greeting. Don't start."

"I'm not the one with the attitude," he said. "Your tone of voice makes your feelings clear."

Alyssa didn't think her tone of voice had been anything but polite, but she refused to be drawn into this familiar argument again. If he couldn't find anything to object to in the words she used, he would criticize her tone. She shook her head and marched past him.

"We can still withdraw the annulment, you know," he said behind her. "It's not too late."

She turned, very much against her will. "Yes, it is."

"I've been hanging with your dad," he said. "He thinks you can still be made to see reason."

"Uh-huh. And was this his advice on how to talk to me?"

He didn't answer. "He also said you weren't seeing anybody."

"Not that it's any of your business. Or his." She didn't wait for a reply and hurried on into the house. Her father was right inside the front door, as if he had been watching the exchange. "Hi, Dad," she said.

"Alyssa," he said curtly. He gave her an absent-minded kiss on the cheek and stepped back to look her over. "It's high time you cut your hair," he said. "You're too old to look like a teenager."

****

"What?" Reid wanted to say something

57

smoother—*I don't believe I heard you correctly*—but he was too surprised.

"Anything come to mind?" Macias was enjoying his confusion. "No? We have evidence suggesting you were the intended target, not Baird."

Reid shook his head. "I've been in town less than two months. I barely know anybody here."

"You knew a lot of people in Chicago, though, yes? Glenn D'Allesandro? Todd Lerum?"

"I don't know anybody by those names. You think somebody wanted to kill me? Am I in danger?"

"I don't know. Maybe. It would be a good idea if you helped us, then, wouldn't it?"

"You said you had evidence…?"

Macias studied him briefly and then picked up his notebook, extracted a photograph, and laid it on the table. It showed a piece of paper with a dark stain near one edge and handwritten words—*Reed Lucas.* The rest was smudged and not entirely legible—was that a 5 or an 8?—but he could make out the pattern of a California license plate.

"Do you recognize the handwriting?"

"No. He misspelled my name."

"He? Who?"

"Whoever. What does this…?"

"It was found stuffed into a drainpipe about a block away from the Canavard office building."

"Conavard," Reid corrected automatically.

"It was on the back of this." Macias handed him another photo.

The picture of a picture was not very clear, but he recognized his own face. It was a candid shot and not quite rectangular, as if it had been cut from a larger image. He didn't know where or when it had been taken. Not enough was visible in the picture to identify anything.

"It was found with a sixteen-inch tire iron that showed traces of blood," Macias continued.

Reid couldn't even begin to sort this all out. "He put the murder weapon in a drainpipe? There must be better ways to dispose of such incriminating evidence."

"He might have been careful to put it where it wouldn't be traced to him, or he might have had to dispose of it in a hurry. Or maybe he's stupid."

"Maybe," Reid said. If the man who had used the tire iron was coming after him, he would prefer to believe he was stupid. After all, he might have killed the wrong man. He had a nasty feeling in the pit of his stomach, to think someone else had died in his place. He hoped there was another explanation.

"Not entirely, though," Macias went on. "No fingerprints on the tire iron or the picture. But fingerprints *were* found in Baird's office, and they don't match anybody who worked for the company or anybody in the system. They were in places a client wouldn't be likely to touch, on the far side of the desk and the arms of the chair, and they were fresh—not blurred, overlapping Baird's, so probably the killer's— and the same prints were on the light switch and the doors of the office and the restroom where the body was found. They aren't on the computer or the phone or the drawers, and nothing seems to be missing from the office, but the ones on the desk are the clearest prints I've ever seen in the field, as if the subject had pressed down hard on the surface. He couldn't have left better prints if he'd tried."

"So…what? He wore gloves to kill Baird and then took them off and sat at his desk? Left his prints on purpose? Trying to get caught?"

The detective shrugged and took the pictures back. He pointed to the scrawled letters and numbers. "Our experts say even though the ink is the same color, there are two different kinds, so probably written at different times, but apparently by the same person."

"My name, misspelled, and a license plate number? It's not mine. I didn't even have a car when Baird was killed, and it's not the rental."

"It belongs to his Mercedes."

Reid shook his head. "I don't understand. The killer wrote down my name and Baird's license plate?"

"At different times. Did you ever drive his car?"

"No. My license was suspended."

"Like that ever stopped anyone."

"It stopped me. The only time I even saw his car was the day of the interview when he took me out for a drink. There was a restaurant with a bar in the office building, but he insisted on this other place."

"So somebody could have seen you in or near the Mercedes?"

"I guess so. I didn't see anybody in the parking garage, but there were people around at the bar, of course."

"What bar?"

Reid thought about it. His memories of that night were not at all clear, except for the part where Alyssa had appeared like an angel of light to roll away the stone of incarceration. "Monkey something? Monkey's Paw?"

Macias, holding his notebook with a pen poised to

write the name, looked up and frowned. "The Monkey Wrench?"

"Maybe, but the sign had a picture of a monkey on it."

"Yes, the Monkey Wrench. You know it's a gay bar?"

"No. I mean, it didn't look like one, especially. I guess I didn't notice."

"Was Baird gay?"

"I wouldn't know. He was married. It wouldn't have been my business."

"But he took you out for a drink and insisted on this particular place? Did he come on to you?"

"No, not at all. He was entirely appropriate and only talked about Conavard, how he started the company and what he wanted to accomplish. He said he liked their…not the drinks, the pretzels maybe? I remember they were hot and salty."

"Did he talk about his wife?"

"Not that I remember."

"That seem odd to you? He's married to this knockout of a woman, and he doesn't even mention her?"

"It was a business meeting."

The detective wrote something in his notebook. "Yeah, right," he said. "I still think the wife has something to do with it."

"That doesn't make any sense," Reid protested. "If Mrs. Baird is the motive, why would the killer have *my* name and picture? And why his license plate number? Anybody at Conavard would know the Mercedes was his car, not mine, and she certainly would."

"Maybe she wanted you both dead," Macias

suggested. "We know she didn't do the deed, but she could have...enlisted someone else. And we can't discount the possibility that Baird hired somebody to kill you and you killed him first."

"But you don't believe that."

"No," Macias said. "It wouldn't explain the license number, but it's more than that. Let's call it instinct. The same instinct tells me Gloria Baird was not a faithful wife." He unfolded a sheet of paper from his notebook and handed it to Reid. It held three columns of names, last name first. He spotted Glenn D'Allesandro's name and searched for and found the other name the detective had mentioned—Todd Lerum. "These are friends, associates, and acquaintances of Mrs. Baird. Take a good look and tell me if you know any of them."

Reid looked up at him instead. "So, when you said you knew we had mutual acquaintances, you were lying?"

"Bluffing," Macias corrected. "It's a legitimate interrogation technique."

"I wasn't under arrest."

"Interview technique," Macias said, keeping his expression neutral. "Take a look," he prompted.

Reid studied each name, but none of them rang a bell. "Gary Smith is a very common name," he said. "I think I knew one in elementary school."

The detective took the paper back and folded it inside his notebook. "What I would like from you now is a similar list. Friends, associates, co-workers, acquaintances, schoolmates—you can skip the elementary grades—the cleaning lady, whoever you can think of. Here and in Chicago."

"Here will be a short list," he said. "Chicago—I don't know if I can remember them all."

"Yes, you can," Macias said, making it sound like an order. "Take your time. Think about it for a day or two."

"And meanwhile somebody might be trying to kill me?"

"Nobody has yet. It's always a good idea to keep your eyes open, of course." He stood, so Reid did too. "I want to thank you for your cooperation, Mr. Lucas," he said formally. He walked to the door and held it open. As Reid went out, Macias said, "I know you don't think much of me, but I'm good at my job. And for what it's worth, I still think you were fucking Glowria Baird." He gave him a mocking smile and added, "Have a nice day."

Chapter Seven

Reid didn't go back to Conavard when he finished early at the job site. Instead he headed to the only other places he was allowed to drive—a DUI class and straight home. He had been a little edgy whenever he was in the office, and especially in the underground parking garage. Too many movies and TV shows had made it seem like a prime location for violent crime. He assumed the killer wouldn't know where he lived and so far hadn't felt unsafe in the apartment, but he kept a nervous eye on the rearview mirror en route. He knew he was safer for being aware of the danger, but that was not how he felt.

He had started working out a few details on his laptop when the doorbell rang.

It was Alyssa, pretty as a picture. Her hair was down, those long, shining locks falling across her shoulders. She had an inviting, clean scent, as if she had just showered, with a hint of vanilla. Her *Zombie Apocalypse Running Team* T-shirt was a little snug, her legs slim and graceful in blue denim.

"To what do I owe the pleasure?" he asked. He said it casually, pretending that it wasn't deeply gratifying to see her—and alone for a change.

"I'm hiding out," she said, which only increased his satisfaction—she saw him as a refuge. "Is this okay? I don't mean to intrude." She glanced around as if she expected to find a party going on or a home improvement project in progress.

"It's fine," he said. "I was working. I could use an excuse for a break."

"You work at home too?"

"Right now, I do. We keep regular office hours, but it's not always a nine-to-five kind of job." He gestured for her to enter and glanced at his watch. "Did you just get off work?"

"Yes. I changed in the locker room and came straight here. I saw your car in the garage, so…"

"Can I get you something to drink?"

"Don't go to any trouble," she said. She stood in the middle of the living room, her hands in her jeans pockets, still looking around.

"Who are you hiding from?" he asked.

"My husband," she said. "My *ex*-husband. I had him served with divorce papers today, and I'd rather he couldn't get hold of me until he has time to calm down."

"You did?" It sounded like a wonderful idea. "Weren't you waiting for a church annulment?"

"I got tired of waiting. This is a no-fault state, and we have no assets to divide, so he has no grounds to contest it."

"Sit down," he said. "I think this enterprising action calls for a celebration." He went into the kitchen and surveyed his options. He wasn't much better prepared than he had been when Jane dropped by, but he could do better than pizza rolls. Cheese and crackers, carrot sticks—light, healthy snacks that wouldn't spoil her dinner. She had to be calorie conscious to keep her slim figure. He added a bottle of white wine and glasses to the tray.

When he carried it into the living room, Alyssa was sitting on the edge of the couch, looking ill at ease. She took her hand away from her mouth quickly, but he guessed she had been biting her fingernails. She looked up at him and relaxed a little, sliding back against the cushions. She was somehow prettier like this, on edge, frowning, more human, more reachable.

"Big step," he said sympathetically.

"Is it okay that I came here? I should have called, at least."

"It's fine. Does Jane know where you are?"

"No. I told her I wasn't coming home, but if she doesn't know where I am, she can't tell."

"She might guess," he suggested.

"He knows our other friends. I thought this would be safest. I'm not afraid of him, y'know, but I don't want the kind of scene he would make." He poured wine into the glasses and held one out to her. Alyssa raised her eyebrows. "AA lost its appeal?"

"It's for cooking," he said, "but this is a celebration."

"Who have you been cooking for? ...Oh, none of my business."

"A few of my neighbors, and two guys from work who wanted to talk about Baird's murder."

"No new ladies in your life? Married or otherwise?"

He shook his head.

"Not looking?" she guessed. "Not over Sarah yet?" Before he could answer, she put a hand on his. "Sorry," she said. The contact was brief and impersonal, but he felt it deeply.

"We're quite a pair," he said.

She took a carrot stick. "You're always feeding me. You're so nice."

He wasn't sure it was a compliment. *Nice* was such a namby-pamby word.

"I won't stay long. When I don't come right home, he'll give up for tonight. He won't lie in wait or anything. He doesn't have the patience." She bit into the carrot and studied him. "So…what are you working on?"

"Control hierarchy for an algorithm…" He trailed off because she had a blank expression on her face.

"Okaaay… Sorry I asked. What happened in Chicago? You had a job, yes? You lost it? The economy?"

"Not entirely."

"Let me guess. The boss's wife." She was joking. She took a healthy swig of wine.

"Not exactly. Close."

"Reid! You are a dangerous man." The doorbell rang. "Are you expecting company?" she asked. "I can leave." She put down her glass and reached for her shoulder bag.

"Stay put," he said. He wasn't expecting anybody, and there certainly wasn't anybody he would rather see. He hoped it wasn't Jane, the ever-present chaperone.

The man who stood outside his door was tall, well-dressed, and fairly good-looking, with a determined chin and narrow blue eyes. His hair was medium brown and a little thin on top. He gave Reid an interested and frankly hostile stare. "I don't believe I've had the pleasure," he said. "Mister…?"

"Reid Lucas," he said automatically. "And you

are…?" Not that he didn't know, hadn't half guessed even before he opened the door.

"Paul Knight." He didn't offer to shake hands. "I know she's here—Alyssa. Aren't you going to invite me in?"

"I don't believe the lady wants to see you right now."

"Oh, you don't? I don't think you know the first thing about her, and you sure don't know me." He shoved his way inside, and Reid managed only to put out an arm to bar his way to the living room. Knight was about to knock it aside when Alyssa came into the entryway.

"Reid," she said. "It's all right. I'll leave with him."

Reid lowered his arm, but he said, "I think you should stay here." Knight would be forced to remain civil in front of a witness, but he might hurt her if he got her alone, even though she had said he wasn't physically abusive. There was always a first time, and she had never divorced him before.

"How did you find me?" Alyssa asked Knight.

"I followed you from the police garage."

"Isn't that a little creepy, even for you? How did you know which apartment?"

"I asked around. You've been here before. This your new boyfriend?" He gestured dismissively toward Reid.

"That would be none of your business."

"You're sleeping with him?"

"I can't imagine any context in which I would ever want to answer that question," she said with great dignity, her voice calm and steady.

"Doesn't look like much," Knight commented.

She didn't rise to the bait. "Where I go and who I see is not your concern."

"You're still my wife."

"Not anymore," she said.

He shook his head. "This civil divorce won't be final for six months, and in the eyes of the church, you always will be."

"It's been a technicality for a long time," she told him.

He turned to Reid. "Did she tell you she's a married woman?"

"She mentioned it."

He glared at Alyssa. "You agreed to wait for the annulment."

"I changed my mind."

"You never could stick to anything," Knight said scornfully and turned back to Reid. "I suppose I have you to thank for this betrayal."

"He has nothing to do with it," Alyssa said.

"Sorry to disappoint you, but we're just friends," Reid confirmed.

"Sure you are. Didn't take long, did it? The ink isn't even dry. Answer me—are you sleeping with him?"

"You'd like that, wouldn't you?" she challenged. "New grounds for your precious annulment. You can't let me go without nullifying me. You can't admit we failed at marriage, like everybody else."

"*I* didn't fail," Knight said. "You were the one who couldn't act like a grownup. You would never admit you were wrong, and honey, you were wrong a *lot*."

"I want you to leave," she said. "Now."

"Here's a shocker for you, sweetheart," Knight said. "At this point I don't care what you want."

"But I do," Reid said. He approached Knight without hesitation, took a fistful of his shirt collar, and escorted him toward the door. Knight sputtered a bit but was too surprised to resist, and Reid had the strength of righteous indignation. He opened the door, shoved him out, and locked it behind him.

Alyssa's mouth was hanging open. "Muh hero," she said, trying to make a joke of it but obviously impressed. "I could have handled him myself," she added, but it sounded weak, mere feminist lip service.

He shrugged. "Bullies are usually cowards," he said, but he was almost as surprised as she was. He knew he couldn't have bested Knight in a serious fight.

They returned to the living room, sat down, and tried to pick up where they had left off, but it was hard to remember what they had been talking about before the interruption.

"I see what you mean," he said. "He's obviously not ready for a calm discussion."

"And I'm not ready to deal with him," she said. "I'm sorry he was rude."

"You're not responsible for him."

"I know, but it's my fault he showed up here." She sighed. "He always made me feel this way—guilty, in the wrong."

"Gaslighting you."

"Right, but…I'm sorry to bring our drama here."

"It's not a problem. What does he do?"

"He works for a biotech company. It's an admin job, dead boring, but it pays well." She nibbled at a piece of buttery cheese and studied Reid.

"Are you okay?" he asked.

"Yeah… After we separated and he applied for the annulment, people told me it was okay for me to date," she said, "but I didn't. I never wanted to—or not enough. It's not like I miss sex. As overrated things go, it's pretty high on the list."

He didn't agree, but no response seemed like the wisest choice.

"Why do men always think you're a slut if you don't want them?" she asked. "Or else a lesbian?"

Reid shook his head. "Ego?"

"Which do you think I am?"

"Neither. I think you made a very sensible decision—to divorce him."

Alyssa sighed. "He was so great when I first met him," she said. "He was always nice to me, as long as I stayed where he wanted me. He didn't mind my working, so I couldn't think of him as a controlling male chauvinist…but I guess he was. He was always trying to put me in my place, even in bed… Don't you hate it when women whine about their awful exes?" She looked at him, but he didn't answer. Silence was better than saying the wrong thing. "I suppose you liked me better when I was married."

"I like you either way," he said lightly. She was watching him intently, and he had trouble holding her gaze. She was so beautiful like this, thoughtful and troubled. It made it hard to think rationally. He looked at his glass and asked, "I didn't have anything to do with your decision, did I?" He took a sip of wine before he met her eyes.

"No," she said, but she averted her gaze.

"We're just friends," he said. It was a statement of

fact, but something other than friendship was shimmering between them. Not sexual tension, or not exactly… Did she feel it too?

"Damn," she said. "Don't do this to me." Without another word, she put her wine glass on the coffee table, rose, and took his hand. She led him into the bedroom. The lush, green view from the large window had never been prettier, but she stood next to the bed, looking only at him. She seemed uncertain what she wanted to do and let go of his hand.

Reid wasn't looking at the view either. He couldn't see anything but her as she skinned off her T-shirt. What was this? Gratitude? Recklessness? "You don't have to do that," he said.

"Apparently I want to." She unhooked her simple white bra.

"Can we slow down a little here?" he asked. He couldn't pretend he wasn't aroused, but if she went any further, it might be too late to stop what might turn out to be a big mistake. It could end what they already had—not that their friendship was anything to brag about, patched together by Jane out of Alyssa's wariness and his longing.

"Coward," she said, but she kept her tone light. She took a step closer and kissed him, an aggressive, challenging kiss with the rich tang of white wine. "What's the matter? You can't handle it when it's attainable?"

He shook his head. "I like…a few preliminaries. I'm not a slam-bang-thank-you-ma'am kind of guy."

Alyssa studied him for a few weighted seconds before she reached back to re-hook her bra. "I'm sorry," she said. "I don't usually throw myself at guys. I'm a little out of practice." She grabbed her T-shirt and started to leave the room.

Reid caught her arm and pulled her close. He kissed her, much more gently than she had kissed him. Her mouth was lush and inviting, promising more.

She pulled back to look at him, surprised. "What kind of preliminaries?" she asked.

He kissed her again. "Hi," he said. "I'm Reid. Nice to meet you."

She managed a self-conscious laugh. "It wasn't that fast."

He put his arms around her. He found the clasp and unhooked her bra. Her skin was so smooth under his hands, as he had long imagined it would be. Her breathing quickened.

"Make up your mind," she said, but the new huskiness in her voice belied the stern words.

"Hush." He kissed her again, holding it long enough to keep her quiet while he cupped her beautiful breasts, as soft as velvet and unbelievably responsive to his touch.

"I know what you think," she said.

"No, you don't," he said and kissed her again.

****

Lying beside Alyssa, Reid touched her face, tracing a line across her cheek. "Wow," he said. He felt relaxed, happy, grateful, at peace with the world. Whatever complications he had anticipated had disappeared.

"Don't be corny," she said.

"Is that what I am? Corny?" He didn't care if she teased him.

Alyssa shrugged. She had covered herself with the

sheet, and he lifted it away. "What?" she said. "It's not as if you've never seen a woman's body before."

"I've never seen *yours* before," he said. He ran a hand over the lovely curve of her hip. There was solid muscle in her compact body, but the skin under his hand was warm and silky.

"Don't," she said and pulled the sheet up again.

Undaunted by the rebuff, he played with her hair, letting the long dark strands slip between his fingers. He stroked the edges of her delicately shaped pink ears, which made her murmur in appreciation, and squeezed the small, scarred lobes—they had been pierced at one time and healed. Every little thing about her was important and fascinating. She was a complicated woman, a tough police officer, but vulnerable underneath. He kissed her. "Thank you," he said.

"For what? You think I was doing you a favor?" She was bristling, but only a little.

"No, but I feel…"

"Obliged? Don't." She rolled away and sat up.

"No," he said, but he did—obliged, grateful, lucky, blessed.

"Oh, stop grinning," she said.

"I can't," he said. "I'm happy." He was also embarrassed and confused, but mostly happy.

"You shouldn't be. You just complicated your life. No, *I* did—and my own."

"Not unless you want to. I won't stalk you or anything."

"That's big of you."

"If it's because of…whatever, that's okay too." He didn't think they had been anywhere near this before Knight showed up. Reid didn't want to believe her ex was the catalyst, but it was the most likely explanation. "I know I'm not every girl's dream."

"Meaning what?" She raised her eyebrows. "You have a good job and a great apartment. Women aren't as obsessed with perfect bodies as you guys."

"So, all in all, my best quality is my apartment?"

"I wouldn't say that. Nice bed, though." She patted the mattress. "You have a certain *je ne sais quoi*…"

She was studying him critically, so he offered, "Jane said I need a haircut." Alyssa ran a hand through his hair. Her fingers sent a shiver down his spine. It was an amazing sensation, almost painfully intense.

"No, I don't think so," she said. "Not yet."

He liked the way her voice made him feel. She bent and kissed him, a much nicer kiss than their first one, but somewhat brisk and impersonal.

"I think I should take a shower," she said. She got quickly out of bed and gathered her clothes.

He didn't say anything except, "Sure." She knew where the bathroom was, and she hadn't asked him to join her. She closed the bathroom door firmly. He supposed she was having second thoughts. He got out of bed too, pulled on his pants, retrieved his shirt from the floor, and buttoned it as he ambled into the kitchen.

He stood in the open refrigerator door, his thoughts scattered. Coffee was his first impulse, and he closed the door and turned on the coffee maker. He had all but forgotten the wine and snacks in the living room. It was early evening, a reasonable supper time, but breakfast had more appeal, maybe because he was used to this scenario playing out in the morning. He heard the shower turn on.

He didn't think he would have time to make

cinnamon rolls from scratch, even with his mother's quick and easy recipe, but he had some of the refrigerated kind and put them in the oven right away. He scrambled the eggs in olive oil. He had a lot of fresh ingredients he could have added, but it was best to keep it simple.

He was right; Alyssa was quick. In no time at all she was standing in the kitchen doorway. Her hair was slightly damp, and she looked…delicious.

"I should go," she said and then, "Oh…" She hesitated, poised for getaway, but realizing he was going to some trouble for her. She glanced at the eggs and raised her eyebrows. "Is it morning already?" she asked.

"You can eat breakfast any time of day," he said. She was still wavering, so he added, "Cinnamon rolls," and pointed to the oven.

She came in slowly and sat at the table. Unlike Jane, she didn't seem to want to crowd him in his own kitchen. He was afraid she would leave after all at the slightest excuse, so he quickly served the eggs and coffee and let the cinnamon rolls wait.

He sat across from her, watched her make random stabs with her fork, and waited for her to say something. She didn't at first. She was very quiet, very still. He was waiting for a brush-off, an exit line. Instead, she sipped her coffee without looking at him and asked, "Where did you learn to make love like that?"

His heart jolted at the word *love,* even as he waited for the criticism her tone promised. "I don't know," he said. "Married women?"

She looked up, exasperated. "You know what I

mean," she said. He didn't. "It was very sweet, Reid, but I don't want you to get hurt. This wasn't casual for you."

"But for you it was." It wasn't a question. He had expected as much. It was a momentary impulse, a rebound fling not meant to go anywhere.

"No," she said, surprising him, "but not in the same way."

"Okay," he said. "Whatever. It's okay. Eat your eggs. The cinnamon rolls will be hot in a few minutes."

"You were right. We should slow this down." She was letting him down easy.

"Okay."

"Stop saying okay," she said. "You might try fighting back."

"What?"

"Stick up for yourself a little."

"Sometimes that leads to... Bad things happen. People get hurt."

"What?" She stared, her lovely lips parted. "You mean like...to women who rejected you? Guys who got you arrested?"

"No, Alyssa, I'm not a serial killer. If I was, I'd start with Detective Macias. But I did get Sarah killed." He didn't tell her he might have gotten Baird killed too. It was beginning to dawn on him that if he had reason to be paranoid, anyone with him, including Alyssa, could be in danger too.

"Did you learn your lesson? Don't mess with married women?"

"It doesn't look like it."

She did eat her eggs while she studied him, maybe thinking about what to say next. Finally, she said,

"What would you say if I asked you to go to church with me?"

It was the last thing he would have expected. "Okay, sure," he said, keeping his tone casual. "I could make brunch after."

"I think you already did," she said. "Good coffee, by the way." She took another sip. "See, there's another good quality—you cook. And you're reasonably neat. You'd make somebody a great husband."

"Jane says girls just want to have fun."

"Jane and Cyndi Lauper. And did you?"

"What?"

"Did you have fun with Jane?"

"I had pizza rolls and *Breaking Bad* with Jane."

"Was it fun?"

"Not very." He remembered how annoyed he had been with her. "She wanted me to go out with her or give her a foot rub or something."

"Or something," Alyssa said.

"You don't think I went to bed with her, do you?"

"I don't know. Not my business. She gets around, but I think she's careful. Was the elevator story true?"

"Yes."

"So, you always go around randomly rescuing damsels in distress?"

"Jane wasn't in distress. Neither were you. I'm sure she could have handled the situation, but the guy was a creep. I couldn't just stand by."

"Uh huh. And she gave you her card and tried to sell you Tupperware?"

"Yes."

"And you thought she would be grateful enough to bail you out of jail?"

"I could only hope. Why the cross-examination? Why don't you believe that's what happened?"

She shook her head. "Sorry. I'm being a cop, I guess. Jane isn't the first person most guys would think of to bail them out."

"Maybe not, but I didn't have a lot of options, and I'm glad I did," he said. "Otherwise, we wouldn't have met." He was afraid she would think he was being corny, but she didn't seem to have noticed.

"And you only had one drink."

"Maybe it was two."

"At least. I'm used to people lying to me," she said. "I'm always looking for the discrepancy in the story."

"You'd make a good detective. It must be hard on relationships, though." He got up and took out the cinnamon rolls.

"Relationships *are* hard," Alyssa said.

"They don't have to be." Reid put the hot, sugary rolls on a plate.

"In what universe?"

"This one." He bent to give her a quick kiss, and before she could react, he offered her the plate of cinnamon rolls. She shook her head, but she took one. They smelled too good to resist.

"I can't begin a new relationship until I understand why the last one failed," she said. She bit into the pastry. "Sinful," she said, as if sin was a good thing.

"I'll make homemade next time," he promised. "And bacon. Or maybe—"

"Stop," she said.

"What?"

"Just stop. I can't do this right now." She took a last gulp of coffee and got to her feet.

"Please don't rush off," he said. "We can do whatever you want, talk about whatever you want to talk about."

She shook her head and turned away, but she took the cinnamon roll with her.

"Don't forget Knight might still be outside," he warned. "Waiting for you."

"I'll be careful," she promised. Resigned, he rose to follow her out. At the door, she kissed him, a casual, dismissive kind of kiss. She tasted of coffee and cinnamon. "Now *I'm* feeling corny," she said. She bit her lip, which made him feel both sympathy and a sexy little thrill. "I'm sorry I...forced the issue."

"It's okay," he said.

She shook her head. "You're so easy. You're like a puppy. It's flattering, but it won't last."

He felt unfairly dismissed but couldn't think of anything to say in his own defense. He had to let her go.

Chapter Eight

Alyssa was patting down a suspect, checking for weapons, a task that called for her full attention, but she was a little distracted. Last night's events had seemed natural at the time, but now she couldn't imagine what she had been thinking. She had taken an enormous leap of faith—or else she had taken leave of her senses.

At first sight she had dismissed Reid as harmless, not sexy, not her type, but he had been a surprisingly physical presence as he escorted Paul out of the apartment. Nothing had changed, but maybe he was a little less harmless than she had thought, a little more interesting? He did have very nice eyes, even if they reminded her of a cocker spaniel's, and he was a fabulous cook.

She had images of him now that she didn't want to have, sense memories, as her actor friends would say. His body was not as soft as she had expected. He was pretty fit compared to the skinhead slob she was frisking and other guys she had been seeing all day. She had wanted to direct him and then hadn't needed to. The way he touched her had made her feel soft and warm, as if her flesh was melting under his hands.

She tugged the suspect's right hand behind him and snapped on the cuff. She remembered Reid's mouth on hers. There was more tenderness in his kisses than she would have expected him to show this soon, if ever.

Could he honestly feel that…for her?

She wrenched the left hand back. "Whoa," the skinhead said. "Easy, sweetheart."

"Officer Sweetheart to you," she said. She shoved his head down and maneuvered him into the back seat.

Ty gave her a look across the top of the car as they got in. "Something bugging you?" he asked.

"Lots of things are bugging me," she said. "Why do these guys think they can get away with this shit?"

****

Two days after Reid delivered his acquaintance list to Detective Macias, Randy Goff rapped on his door and opened it without waiting for a response. "Hey, uh…Lucas?"

Since Baird's death, and without any discussion, everyone at Conavard had started closing their office doors except when they expected a client. It was an odd reaction, because Baird had been killed in the men's room, but it was universal. Reid preferred the greater privacy when he was working, but it was harder to get to know his co-workers. Conversation in the restroom, the small staff kitchen, the hallways, and at the reception desk was quieter, more subdued than before, and often consciously skirted the one topic of concern to everyone.

Reid turned away from his computer screen, his mind still on his work, and said, "Hi."

"Yeah, hi," Goff said. He stepped in, closed the door behind him, and got right to the point. "What did you tell the police about me?"

"Nothing," Reid said. He didn't know anything to tell. "Detective Macias wanted a list of everybody I know here, and all the Conavard employees were on it, but that's it. He asked some very general questions about everybody, but he didn't single anybody out. Why?"

"They made me come in to the police station. The detective treated me like a suspect." A whining note had crept into Goff's voice.

"Me too. Probably all of us. I don't think it means anything. The dude's kind of a jerk."

"He, uh…asked some pretty personal stuff. With you too?"

"Like was I sleeping with the boss's wife?"

Goff looked relieved. "Yeah, like that."

"Possible motive," Reid said neutrally.

"He asked me about you too, what I thought of you, who I'd seen you with. He didn't ask much about anybody else. Does it mean we're the main suspects?"

"Mrs. Baird used to live in Chicago, so he thought we might have a connection. But I'm sure everybody's a suspect at this point."

"The thing is…" Goff moved closer, leaned in confidingly, and lowered his voice. "I kind of was."

"You were kind of what?"

"You know, boinking Gloria Baird."

"Really?" Reid caught himself studying his co-worker, wondering what she might see in him.

"Don't tell anyone," Goff cautioned.

"Why did you tell *me*?" He could guess—he needed to tell somebody, to brag, and who better than the newcomer he knew least and who had Macias as a common antagonist?

Goff shrugged.

"Did you tell the police?" Reid asked.

"No way."

"You know if they find out you lied, you'll be in worse trouble."

"They won't find out. They're basically incompetent, you know. If you tell them what I said, I'll deny it. This conversation never happened."

"What if they ask her?"

"They won't. She's overwhelmed with grief, blah blah blah. She was out of town the weekend of the murder, you know, so nobody missed him when he didn't come home Saturday night. She has an alibi, and it isn't me. The cop asked me for a sample of my handwriting too. What's that about?"

Reid shrugged. He didn't know whether he should tell people he might be a target. Macias hadn't cautioned him not to talk about anything they had discussed, but he shrank from revealing something that would sound overdramatic and silly, as if he were asking for attention and sympathy. All he wanted was to stay under the radar and get from one day to the next.

After Goff left, Reid considered him as a possible suspect. If he was involved with Mrs. Baird, he might have a motive to kill the boss, but if *he* was the target…Goff knew the Mercedes belonged to Baird, and he wouldn't mistake him for Reid. As for the third side of the triangle, Gloria might have hired somebody to kill her husband, but she didn't even know Reid.

****

"Emerson?" It was Jane's voice on the line. "Would you do me a favor?"

"Not if you keep calling me Emerson." He turned away from the computer screen and gave the call his full attention.

She giggled. "Sorry. Reid. Could you maybe swing

by the apartment? It's on your bus route, isn't it?"

"On *a* bus route," he said.

"It's just Liss wanted some things, and I'm going to be like stuck here for a few hours." She didn't say where *here* was, but she wasn't working. The schools and libraries were closed for a holiday he had never heard of, although he knew who Cesar Chavez was. "Y'know, they gave her something and told her not to drive."

A jolt of alarm surged through him. "Wait—what?"

"Oh," she said vaguely. "I guess you didn't know. She got hurt."

"What!"

"It's no big deal," Jane assured him. "She did you a favor once, so I didn't think you'd mind taking her what she asked for. It's only a couple things from the drug store."

Refusing wasn't possible, but he was nervous about going to the Ocean View apartment without being sure he wasn't shadowed by Baird's killer. The last thing he wanted to do was endanger Alyssa and Jane, and the sick feeling in the pit of his stomach grew out of the fear that he had already done so and someone—Paul Knight or whoever had been carrying the picture of "Reed Lucas"—had hurt Alyssa.

****

The door was open behind the sturdy screen door. He rang the doorbell and heard a distant shout he took for "Come in." The screen door wasn't locked. He entered and looked around. Both bedroom doors were open. He glanced into one—empty, cluttered, full of color, probably Jane's—and walked into the other.

He had never been in here before. The room was neat and pretty, with blue curtains and a queen-size bed with a fluffy white comforter folded at the foot. Alyssa lay on the bed, propped against the pillows. She had the beginnings of a spectacular shiner, and her nose was swathed in bandages. "Oh, ouch," he said.

"Hi," she said. Her voice was very nasal.

"Who did this to you?" he asked. He wanted to know who to direct his rage toward or whether he should feel the guilt of his own responsibility.

"It was an accident," she said, but it sounded more like *ad accidet*. He approached the bed and handed her the paper bag from the pharmacy—the prescribed Percocet, a decongestant, adhesive tape, and three Almond Joy candy bars. "I've had the worst luck sids you showed up."

"Is it broken?" he asked, all sympathy. He bent and kissed her forehead and pretended not to notice her momentary flinch.

She closed her eyes briefly. "It was," she said wearily. "They fixed it." She opened the bag and started taking things out. "Thacks," she said. "How much do I owe you?" She peered at the receipt, but had trouble focusing. She pointed to her shoulder bag, abandoned near the closet.

He shook his head. The amount was negligible, with only a ten-dollar copay for the prescription. Being here with her was worth much more. "What happened?" he asked.

"Accident," she repeated. "Guy was on beth, didn't mean to hurt anybody, took a random, wild swig. Stuff happens."

"Your job is too dangerous."

"Somebody has to do it."

Reid couldn't help smiling. She sounded like a joke, and her face was damaged, but she was still beautiful, to him at least. When she wasn't talking, he couldn't help thinking about what was under her clothes, on this occasion her uniform pants and a short-sleeved green blouse with buttons down the front. Her uniform shirt probably had blood on it. He was oddly happy, even excited. He wasn't glad she had been hurt, but it could have been so much worse, and now he had an opportunity to nurture her in any way she would allow. He was also relieved because her injury had happened on the job and had nothing to do with his involvement with her.

"You should put ice on it," he advised. He didn't wait for her to argue or agree—he went into the kitchen and opened the freezer. A bag of frozen peas would do. He wrapped it in a dish towel and brought it to her with a glass of water. She took a Percocet, put the peas against her bruised eye, and slid down. Reid straightened the pillow under her head and tugged the comforter over her. "Need anything else?" he asked.

"Doe. I'm going to sleep. Thack you." She gave him a vague smile and closed her eyes. He wanted to kiss her, but restraint was the wiser choice.

He returned to the kitchen and checked the cupboards, surveying the cookware and possible ingredients. He didn't find much, but he remembered seeing an Italian market nearby, within walking distance. He would cook while she slept. She needed something nourishing, easy to eat, and flavorful, even though she wouldn't be able to taste much.

He left the apartment quietly. It was nice out,

Southern California spring, dry and warm, the sky starkly clear even after most of the color had faded out with the sun. He didn't see anybody near the apartment, and the two cars parked in front appeared empty. The market was on a busier street, and he studied each unfamiliar face, as if he would know someone capable of murder on sight. He hoped Macias would make an arrest soon because he didn't like feeling this way. He wanted to enjoy what was happening now. Alyssa needed him.

The Italian market was new and modern, the display cases clean and shining, and everything was inviting—pasta, fresh produce, wines, pastries. Gregorio's specialized in Italian cuisine, but the owner was a Latina with fat black pigtails and a welcoming smile. He dismissed prosciutto and plump Italian cookies and selected the makings for a savory bean soup, spinach gnocchi, salad, and a rich dessert. He could make do with a few pots and pans, a large bowl, and the blender Jane used for her smoothies, but he bought a disposable pastry bag and paper muffin cups too.

The preparation took more than an hour, an interlude alone in the half-familiar white kitchen, focused on a labor of love. He loved to cook for this woman. Her approval wasn't easy to win, but well worth the trouble when it came. He had read that most men viewed sex as a way to make a connection more than to express one. Cooking served the same purpose for him. Every time Alyssa ate something he prepared for her, she took a part of him and gave part of herself to him, a gift freely given, no strings attached. Imagine cooking for her every day!

****

Dinner was nearly finished when Jane got home. She slammed the door, apparently not thinking Alyssa might be asleep. She came at once to the kitchen door, attracted by the light and sounds and smells, calling, "Liss?" in a high, surprised voice. She stopped dead when she saw him. "Oh!" she said.

"Hello, Jane."

"You're cooking," she said and grinned, pleased. She moved in to look over his shoulder. "Ooh, what is this? Dessert?"

She stretched out a finger, and he shoved her hand away. "Don't touch," he said, sticking up for himself as Alyssa had advised.

"It looks yummy. What is it?"

"Mascarpone and dark chocolate cream."

"Mascarpone? Sounds like an Italian gangster."

"It's cheese, like a cream cheese. Back up. You're in my light."

She tilted her head toward the bedrooms. "Is she okay?"

"Sleeping, I think."

"Well, she'd better wake up and smell the mas-car-pone. I'm starving." She left the room, and Reid hurried to add the finishing touch of chocolate curls. He put the dessert in the refrigerator and heard Jane's laughter from the bedroom. Alyssa must be awake.

He found a small silver tray and arranged servings of the soup and gnocchi with a napkin and silverware. Instead of a full salad he sliced tomato and avocado—anything crunchy might jar her nose. A glass with ice cubes would be more elegant than a can of pop but might be harder for her to drink from. A straw would be best, but he didn't find any. At the last minute, he decided against letting the dessert wait. He wanted her to get the full effect all at once.

The bedroom door was open. Alyssa was propped against the pillows again with the makeshift icepack to her cheek, and Jane sat on the bed near her feet. "Wow," Jane said. "Supper in bed."

Alyssa's lips parted in pleased surprise. "I coulda god up," she said, but he could tell she liked the pampering. He nodded to Jane to clear the bedside table and set the tray on it. "Chocolate," Alyssa said reverently. "My favorite."

"Why do women crave chocolate?" Jane asked him. "You said you knew."

"Biology," he said as he pulled the straight, blue-cushioned chair close to the bed and sat down. He couldn't remember the exact reason, not when he was watching Alyssa, her eyes a little blurred with sleep and painkillers, her hair soft and loose on her shoulders, her poor damaged nose muffled with gauze.

"Don't thick you're going to get lucky," she said as she lifted the bowl of soup onto her knees. "I'm dot in the mood."

"I wouldn't dream of it," he said. He matched her light tone, but Jane gave him a questioning look.

"Hey," she said. "Are you two…?"

She was asking Alyssa, who turned to Reid for the answer, maybe curious about what he would say. "We're taking it slow," he said. He had assumed women, best friends, roommates would confide in each other about such things. That Jane didn't know must mean something. Yet Alyssa sat here and let him answer the question, let Jane see the smile she gave him.

"I saw him first," Jane pointed out.

"You didn't wad him," Alyssa said carelessly.

"But he cooks."

He took a deep breath. "Ladies!" They both looked at him. "Would you please not discuss me as if I wasn't here?"

"Oh, Reid!" Jane cried, holding her arms out as if for a hug. "Are you here?"

He ignored her. "Careful, it's hot," he told Alyssa as she raised the soup spoon to her mouth. She blew gently on it and tasted it cautiously.

"Tastes good," she said. "I *ab* hungry."

"What is this?" Jane asked, pointing to the gnocchi. "It looks disgusting."

"Don't eat it, then," he said. He cut off a morsel and held it out to Alyssa on the fork.

"Are you going to feed be?" she asked, amused.

"No. Just try this and tell Jane how disgusting it isn't."

"It's green," Jane said.

"Delicious," Alyssa said.

Jane reached for a dumpling and Reid said, "Get your own."

"You're getting awfully bossy," she said. She rose and headed for the kitchen.

"So, you'll be out on sick leave for a while?" he asked Alyssa.

"A few days."

"Longer than that, surely."

"You cad keep a tough cop like me down for long," she said.

The boast made him smile because she looked and

sounded so pathetic.

Jane was back in a minute with two plates of gnocchi. She gave Reid one and perched on the bed with hers. She speared a dumpling and took a bite. "Okay," she said. "It's not too disgusting."

"Why, thank you. What a lovely compliment."

"He's getting snarkier all the time," she told Alyssa.

"He's sweet," she countered and took his hand. "He slaved over a hot stove for us. He keeps doing it. We owe him big time." Talking about him as if he wasn't there was much less annoying with her hand in his.

"You don't owe me anything," he said. "I like to cook."

"I could give him a discount on Tupperware," Jane suggested.

Alyssa rolled her eyes. "I know!" she cried. "We'll give him a tour of the city, all the tourist attractions, the whole works. He can't drive, and he—"

"You can go a lot of places on the bus," Reid objected.

"And have you?" Alyssa asked.

"I've mostly been working," he said, trying not to sound defensive. "Trying to hang onto this job. I've explored Crown Ridge a little, but—"

"We'll plan everything," Alyssa said.

"Hey, yeah," Jane said, getting into the spirit. "I'm sure your Brookfield Zoo is fabulous, but I bet we have a few things you don't in ours."

He would have loved to spend a whole day sightseeing with Alyssa, but why did Jane always have to be included? Because of what had happened the one time he and Alyssa were alone? Was that it? Was she afraid it would happen again? And would it be so awful if it did?

While they listed possible destinations, he considered his options. It was as if he was a teenager again, with a huge, heartfelt crush and unable to think of anything else. She had objected to the idea that she had been doing him a favor—she wanted it as much as he did, so… Maybe she wanted him to make a move, assert himself. But he had promised not to stalk her and didn't want to put himself in the same category as her ex.

She enjoyed the food, but she didn't eat much of the gnocchi or salad. She did finish her soup and dessert and drank the soda pop—her mouth was probably dry.

"More soup?" he asked, and she shook her head. She'd had a hard time, and her eyelids were drooping again. "Go back to sleep," he suggested. "We'll finish our dinner in the kitchen."

Jane immediately gathered the dishes and left the room, and Reid gave Alyssa the kind of kiss he wouldn't want her roommate to see. "Ouch," she said, but with a forgiving smile.

In the kitchen, he reheated the soup and set the table for two. "What does slow mean?" Jane asked. "Do I still have a chance?"

"I thought you wanted to have fun. I'm not fun."

"No," she agreed, all too quickly, "but you could be if you tried. And you cook. Do you like to dance?"

"I *can* dance," he said noncommittally. He wasn't sure if she was flirting. "Why?" he asked and then, unable to resist, "Does Alyssa like to dance?"

"All women like to dance. Men never dance once

they've… Oh!"

"What?"

"You and Alyssa," she said. "She may be taking things slow, but you're already gone."

"Is it that obvious?"

"Pret-ty obvious," she said.

****

When Alyssa woke up, Jane was hovering in the doorway. "Reid is in love with you," she said bluntly. "I thought he was just…"

Alyssa shook her head. "He has a crush on me. He has a thing for married women. We'll see how long it lasts now that I'm getting divorced." She sat up carefully, feeling much less fuzzy but still tired. Against her better instincts, she let her mind linger on the way Reid had looked at her—it was more than sympathy, more than physical desire, and it wasn't as if she was very desirable right now.

"I did see him first," Jane reminded her. "I asked him to have a drink with me. You thought he was a con man."

"And you thought he was gay," she countered.

Jane giggled. "Not really. He sure can cook. There's lots left. D'ya want any more?"

"No." She stretched and slid to the edge of the bed. "I think I'll take a long, hot bath and go back to bed."

"Need any help?"

"No, thanks. I'm fine."

"Okay. Have sweet dreams." Jane started to leave but turned back at the door. "We know he will," she said mischievously.

Chapter Nine

Alyssa was back at work in two days, her eye still very colorful, but only a Band-Aid on the bridge of her swollen nose. To her disgust, she was assigned to desk duty "for a while." Apparently, she didn't present enough of a macho image.

On Thursday Reid called and asked if she wanted to go dancing Friday or Saturday night.

"Dancing?" she echoed blankly. He had called on the landline—he had her cell number in his phone, but she had never officially given it to him—and she stood awkwardly in the hall, trying to make sense of this unexpected development.

"Like with music?" he prompted.

"You're asking me out on a date?"

"Yes."

"What would be the point?" she asked bluntly. "When we've already…"

"Alyssa—"

"Sex is all men want when they—"

"That's not true."

"You're a romantic. Or very naïve."

"Do you want to go dancing with me or not?"

"My face is still messed up. People will think you beat me."

"We'll go to a dimly lit place," he promised.

"What kind of dancing are we talking about?" she

asked, still suspicious. Did dimly lit mean some murky club and a grope fest?

"What kind do you like?" he hedged. "You might know of better places to go than I do, but one of the guys at work told me about the Aurora ballroom where they have a real band and do swing and Latin."

"Who are you?" she demanded. She wasn't entirely joking.

He laughed anyway. "The thing is, we could walk to one of the bars or clubs around here, but if you want to go to the Aurora, you'll have to drive. It's damned inconvenient, but I still can't drive everywhere."

"Drunk driving kills," Alyssa said unsympathetically, "so don't whine about it."

"I'm not," he said. "I'm just sorry to inconvenience you."

"Again," she said heartlessly, but her voice softened as she added, "I don't mind driving. It sounds like fun. Dancing I mean." She still didn't understand his motives, but it was worth a try.

****

It *was* fun. Reid was grateful to Jane for the suggestion, and so glad he had taken the chance. Alyssa had a tendency to try to lead, but she eventually loosened up a little, and she was light and graceful in his arms. Perhaps a few hard looks were sent in his direction, but her face wasn't so bad anymore. The bruise was starting to fade, and the flesh-colored Band-Aid wasn't too obvious. She had her hair coiled on top of her head, leaving her shoulders bare. Her sleeveless dress was knee-length with a fitted bodice and flared skirt. The color, what he believed was called teal, was a good choice with her dark hair.

Between dances they sat at a small table in a poorly lit corner. "You can have a drink if you want to," she told him. "You're not driving."

"No," he said, offering no explanation. "But if you want to, I'll drive you home."

She raised her eyebrows. "You're planning to break the law with a police officer in the car?"

"Would you bust me?"

She shrugged and raised a hand to beckon a waiter. She ordered an apple-ginger sparkler, and Reid asked for a cranberry soda, which Alyssa said was a child's drink. He reminded himself she liked to tease her friends. She sipped hers and studied him over the rim of the glass.

"I can't figure you out," she confessed.

"I know the feeling."

She raised her eyebrows. "I know things about you I don't want to know."

"Good things or bad things?"

"Both. You didn't tell me a few things you should have mentioned."

"Like…?"

"You knew Mrs. Baird in Chicago?"

"No, I didn't. You've been talking to Macias."

"Not directly, but I heard things."

"What you heard is out of date. I never met her before I came to Carroll City."

"Are you sure?"

"I think I would remember. If you think I'm a suspect…"

"No, of course not," she said.

"As a matter of fact, Macias doesn't think I am either, at this point. But whatever happens, don't go out with him."

She blinked. "Who? Macias? He's married."

"So?"

She shook her head. "Jane said you would make a good husband, but you wouldn't. No respect for marriage vows."

"I don't have a good answer to that, but I like to think I would respect my own."

Alyssa glanced around at the room full of sitting and dancing couples. "I still say all men want is sex," she said cynically. "Anyway…what happened the other night…"

He tried to think of the right thing to say, but nothing presented itself.

"I don't want you to think it will happen again, but it was…special. You're probably exactly what I needed after Paul, but that's not a basis for a lasting relationship."

"Okay," he said, but he was afraid she wouldn't like it.

She didn't. She gave an exasperated sigh and took another sip of her sparkler.

"Where did you learn to dance?" he asked to distract her. He didn't want to have a serious conversation. He wanted to gaze at her lovely, bruised face and her soft, white shoulders. The dress hugged her curves in an inviting but not suggestive way.

"Oh, dance lessons in high school mostly. The father-daughter dance was a big deal, and I had to keep up with dear old Dad."

"Was he proud of you following in his footsteps?"

"Hard to tell," she said. She had a closed-off expression now, but finally she confessed, "We aren't on very good terms these days."

"Why not?"

"He took Paul's side. Y'know, the annulment and everything. He thinks I should have tried harder to make the marriage work. Tough it out and be a good little wifey. Quit if he wanted me to, have a baby for him. Be a real woman."

"That's not what a real woman is," Reid said.

"Thank you," she said. "I have to hand it to my father, though, you know. He practices what he preaches. He was faithful to my mom all these years— at least I think he was—and now he's taking care of her. Better or worse, sickness and health…"

"She's at home?"

"Yes. I couldn't do it myself, so maybe he's right. I'm a selfish bitch. I would put her in a nursing home."

He shook his head, but he knew nothing he said would help.

"I'm a good cop, though," she said, brightening a little.

"I'm sure you are." He didn't tell her what Macias had said. *Consider the source.*

"Anyway, I remembered what you said, last time I saw her."

"What did I say?"

"You know, about why she doesn't recognize me. I didn't try to explain who I was. I held her hand and remembered how she used to comfort me when I was sick. When I got up to leave, she said—" She broke off, unable to go on.

Reid put a hand on hers, as she had done for him when she asked if he was over Sarah. "It's okay," he said. He didn't know what he meant, but he had to say something.

Alyssa straightened, slipped her hand out from under his, and took a sip of her drink. "She said I reminded her of her little girl."

"See? She remembers you, but she can't make the connection with this beautiful grownup woman. All parents must feel that way sometimes. 'Where did my cute baby go?' "

"I bet you were, too," she said. "Little chubby-cheeked Emerson."

"It's Reid."

"You didn't say how *your* mother died. Did she die at home?" She had a half-envious, half-resentful expression.

He shook his head. "In a hospital. Very quickly. I didn't get to say goodbye."

"Sorry," she said automatically but not insincerely. "My mother's gone too. I guess it's hard either way."

"Yes, it is." He took a sip of his drink. It did taste sort of like a child's drink. "Are you about ready for another dance?"

"Beats polite conversation," she said.

****

When Alyssa pulled into Reid's assigned space in the apartment building parking garage, he asked, "Want to come up for a cup of coffee or something?"

"Coffee?" she said dubiously.

"You like my coffee."

"Or I was only being polite," she said, but he didn't think she meant it. When was she ever polite? She studied him. "If you do anything I don't like, I'll beat the crap out of you," she warned.

"Or you could use your words."

"What?"

"If I start to cross a line, tell me." She was still hesitant, so he leaned over and kissed her goodnight. He put as much into it as he dared in light of her recent facial injuries. Her hair started to come loose from its clips, and a stray lock tickled his cheek.

"Okay," she said.

"What?"

"Let's go upstairs and…have coffee."

****

Alyssa propped herself on one elbow and studied him. "What is it with you?" she asked. "Jane says you're in love with me, but you can't be. You barely know me."

"You don't want me to know you," he said. "You're very guarded."

"Oh, yeah, Mr. Psychiatrist?"

"Okay," he said mildly, humoring her.

"Is that your favorite word?"

"No…synchronicity. What's yours?"

"Counterintuitive," she said promptly.

"Ah, okay," he said. "Now I know *all* about you."

Alyssa punched him in the shoulder, not hard.

Reid laughed. "Use your words," he said.

"Rap sheet," she obliged. "Misdemeanor. Disorderly conduct."

"Embedded systems," he countered. "Gap analysis. Portability."

"You are so *boring,*" she said.

"At least I don't get hit in the face by meth addicts." He touched her cheek gently.

She didn't wince, but she held her breath.

"Are you sure Knight didn't hit you?" he asked.

"I told you what happened."

"No, I mean…ever. You act like you expect me to hurt you."

"I have a broken nose."

"Okay. I'll try not to touch your face, but damn, it's so pretty!"

"Oh, yeah, I'm gorgeous," she said. "Especially right now." She sat up and grabbed her bra.

"Don't go away mad," he said.

"I'm not mad," she said. "I have to go home. I'll be back in the morning."

"You will?"

"Yes." She hooked her bra and leaned over to kiss him. "We're going to church."

Chapter Ten

St. Anthony's wasn't as spectacular as the Greek Orthodox church in Jane and Alyssa's neighborhood, but it had an almost old-fashioned, intimate charm of its own. Reid was not a stranger to Catholic ritual, but Alyssa was clearly at home here. She was dressed more conservatively than she had been the night before, in a simple navy skirt and long-sleeved blouse, her hemline well below the knee and her figure masked by the soft drape of the fabric.

He stood beside her at the door of St. Anthony's and tried not to stare, while she dipped her fingers into the holy water font and crossed herself. He followed her down the center aisle, impressed by the stained-glass windows and beautiful arches in this small and otherwise modern building. The nave was about half full of people, with no empty seats on the aisle except in the front rows. Alyssa murmured to a young black woman about halfway down, and she rose to let them pass.

He stood when Alyssa stood, knelt when she knelt, but he knew better than to join the communicants at the altar. She did everything with a grave concentration which he did his best to match. It was the last Sunday of the Lenten season, and the sermon was about giving up the things that would disappoint God, the selfish or self-destructive things that should be given up permanently, not for only a few weeks.

"Did that make you uncomfortable?" she asked as they left.

"Not at all. This isn't my first time."

"First time?"

"At a Catholic mass," he clarified.

"No, I meant the sermon." He didn't understand, and she added, not quite accusingly, "Thou shalt not commit adultery."

"Oh," he said.

"It's not only immoral," she pointed out. "It's dangerous."

"Okay," he said.

"Okay again. Okay what?"

"I'll give it up for Lent. It's not like I roamed the streets hunting for wives to poach. I just fell in love with women who happened to be married."

"Once maybe. Several times is a pattern."

He shrugged. "So many women are unhappy in their marriages."

"Uh-huh. Maybe because they're married to men."

"Yes, most of them are. So…what is a nice Catholic girl like you doing with a reprobate like me?"

"Are you a reprobate?" she asked. "Or a sad, misguided guy, looking for Mrs. Goodbar?"

Reid shrugged again and, to change the subject, asked, "What did *you* give up for Lent?"

"French fries," she said with a sigh. "Don't laugh—it's tough to get anything but fast food on the job."

****

Reid led Alyssa into his apartment with a welcoming flourish.

"You don't have to feed me," Alyssa demurred, as she followed him into the kitchen.

"But you know I enjoy cooking for you."

"I am hungry," she admitted.

"I like a woman with a good appetite," he said approvingly.

"How long will this take?" she asked.

"Forty minutes tops," he promised. He had been mulling over brunch choices since she first mentioned going to church. He'd had no trouble coming up with ideas, but he had too many good options to choose from. She had barely touched her scrambled eggs, so he'd considered French toast, pancakes, or waffles instead, but he *did* like eggs, in all their variety, and the presentation could make all the difference. His job was to make them irresistible. Besides, it was nearly Easter, and eggs were fraught with symbolism, suggesting fertility, spring, rebirth, and sacrifice. He had opted for his childhood favorite, Swiss eggs. If she had given up meat for Lent, he could have left out the sausage.

He set right to work and preheated both ovens, one to 325° for the eggs and the other to 400° for the muffins. He had promised to make cinnamon rolls "next time," but the words could mean whatever he wanted them to—next time he served cinnamon rolls he would make them from scratch. Alyssa liked them but she might appreciate a healthier choice. Banana bread, corn muffins, rugelach with fruit filling…? Orange honey muffins had won out in the end.

Coffee, orange juice, and fruit would fill out the menu. Even this time of year, plenty of fresh fruit was available in Southern California, and he settled on a bowl of mostly berries and banana slices.

"What can I do to help?" she asked.

"Set the table?" He pointed. "Plates, bowls, juice glasses. Silverware here." He opened the drawer. "If you're sure you want to help, you can sift the dry ingredients for the muffins. Or you can sit there and look beautiful. Either way works for me."

"Stop saying I'm beautiful when I look like a prizefighter. A losing prizefighter."

"You know what you should give up for Lent?" he asked.

"Yeah, yeah, I know. But I can't. It's part of my basic personality." She started setting the table, and Reid put out the sifter, flour, baking powder, and salt for her before he put the sausage in a saucepan on the stove and mixed cream, mustard powder, and salt for the eggs, and the egg, honey, orange peel, orange juice, milk, and vegetable oil for the muffins.

Alyssa stopped sifting to watch him for a minute. "I don't know how you can do three things at once," she said. "That's what stumps me about cooking. I'm more of a one course at a time gal."

"You're a grazer," he guessed. "Coordinating everything isn't hard, but it does take practice." He took a fork and broke up the sausage as it began to brown, filling the kitchen with a meaty fragrance, and then greased the baking dish. "I wasn't sure you liked eggs," he said, "but Jane said you weren't a picky eater, and I think you'll like these anyway."

"Is that what she said? I'm not a picky eater? I'll eat anything as long as somebody else cooks it is what she meant. Almost anything," she corrected. "Not oily fish like sardines, and I don't think I want to try insects or snails."

"I've heard fried grasshoppers are tasty, but I haven't tried them. Snails sound better in French—I'll make you some nice Helix pomatia with garlic butter some time."

"You are a very strange man," she said.

"Oh? What does that tell us about *you*?"

"I like strange men? Anyway, we've been planning our sightseeing tour. This week would be best, because Jane is off for spring break, but of course everywhere will be more crowded. Otherwise it would be difficult, because I work most weekends and you both work Monday through Friday. I don't have any accumulated vacation time, and I don't suppose you do either, with a new job."

"I could take a day off any time," he said, "as long as I'm getting the work done. If Jane couldn't get off, maybe you and I could…"

Alyssa had a forbidding expression. "No," she said. "We are not excluding Jane."

"You do have some weekends off?" he asked, changing the subject. "Like today?"

She shook her head. "I traded shifts. I have to work later. So, is Tuesday or Wednesday good for you? What would be best would be both days, because we have a lot on our list, but that might be too much to ask."

"Tuesday," he said, "and we'll see about Wednesday." She was finished sifting the dry ingredients, and he took the bowl from her and added the contents of another.

"Do you ever get mixed up?" she asked. "Pour from the wrong bowl?"

"No," he said, "but I don't usually have someone as pretty as you to distract me."

"Oh, stop," she said crossly. "I'm not in the mood to flirt with you."

"Is that what you think I'm doing? Flirting? I was only stating a fact."

"I'm not pretty. Even without the bruises, I'm just ordinary. 'Interesting' maybe, but not pretty."

"Who told you *that*?" He suspected Paul Knight or maybe her father.

"The mirror."

"Then you need a new mirror, cuz that one's lying to you."

Alyssa gave him a playful nudge. At least she had stopped scowling and was in fact almost smiling. "You know what I like about you?" she asked.

"Pray tell."

"You never call me honey or babe."

"This from a woman who called me moron on first meeting."

"I didn't call you a moron. I called you a genius."

"Sarcastically." He turned off the burner under the sausage and drained it.

"Ironically. Also, I liked the bean soup."

"I'll make you some more," he promised. Appreciating his cooking was definitely the way to his heart. He knew something else she liked, but he wasn't going to bring it up.

"What *are* you making?" she asked. She had been hovering close, but now she took a step back and surveyed the entire workspace.

"Swiss eggs," he said. He placed the sausage in the baking dish and topped it with cheddar cheese.

"Swiss? Why Swiss? You're not using Swiss cheese. Are they neutral or run like a fine watch?"

"Now you sound like Jane," he said. He didn't have to answer the question because Alyssa's phone warbled softly.

"Sorry," she said and walked into the hall to take the call. He didn't try to eavesdrop, but as he dotted the cheese with butter, he heard her say, "Yes, and what's it to you?" She was back almost immediately. "I should have turned it off," she said apologetically.

"It's okay," he said. "Is something wrong?"

"No," she said, but she had a closed-off expression again. *What's it to you* might mean nothing—hadn't she said the same thing to him once? He was sure she would say it to Jane. She could be prickly, suspicious— it was an occupational hazard. He poured half of the cream mixture over the cheese and butter. "Curiouser and curiouser," Alyssa said.

He took the carton of eggs out of the refrigerator and suddenly tossed one in her direction, just to see what she would do.

She caught it deftly, very pleased with herself.

"Whoa," he said. "Ever play baseball?"

"Sure. In the streets as a kid and in high school."

"You were a tomboy?"

"I threw like a girl," she said.

"So did Babe Didrikson. So, if I called you Babe…"

She tossed the egg back to him. He caught it one-handed, but the shell broke, and slimy albumen dripped from his fingers. "Oops," said Alyssa, unable to suppress a smile.

He set the rest of the eggs on the table and turned to the sink to wash his hands, trying to hold onto his dignity.

Repentant, she grabbed a paper towel and cleaned up what had dropped on the floor.

"You started it," she said.

"Yes, I did," he admitted. He handed her the bowl of muffin mixture and a spoon. "Pour this into the muffin cups," he instructed. "About two-thirds full."

"You're very trusting," she said.

"I'm giving you the easiest parts," he pointed out, "but I do appreciate your help." He began beating the eggs. "It will go faster this way." She didn't start right away but watched him with something like admiration. "It's all in the wrists," he said.

"All done," she said a minute later and held out the muffin tin for inspection. He gestured for her to put it on the sink and poured the frothy eggs into the baking dish. She watched while he drizzled the remaining cream mixture onto the eggs and slid the dish into the top oven.

"These too?" she asked, pointing to the muffin tin.

"Not yet." He peeled and drained an orange, put a section in each muffin cup, sprinkled them with sugar, and put the tin in the bottom oven. He set the timer for the minimum time, twenty minutes.

"Now what?" she asked. She was a little flushed from the oven heat and had a smudge of flour on her nose.

"Hold still," he said. She flinched when he touched her nose. He didn't think he'd hurt her, but she grabbed his hand anyway.

"Flour," he said.

"Oh," she said, but she didn't let go of his hand. She was very close, and she was holding him there. He kissed her. "You are such a bad boy," she said.

****

Alyssa was lying in his arms, which she had never done before, her head on his chest, nestled under his chin. He stroked her dark, velvety hair. "We have to stop doing this," she said.

"Why?" he asked.

"Because it isn't real."

"Seemed pretty real to me."

"*We* aren't real," she said. "It's like some dumb *Playboy* fantasy or a bad movie."

"Alyssa," he said, knowing he was treading dangerous ground. "I know this isn't any of my business or anything, but how many men have you been with?" She thought sex was overrated, and maybe it was, but maybe she didn't have much basis for comparison.

"Definitely none of your business," she said.

"Okay."

"Okay," she repeated, mocking him.

"Was it your ex who called earlier?" he asked.

"Also none of your business," she said, but after a moment she added, "He didn't mind my working, but now I realize he kept me from getting my college degree. I was a semester away from finishing when he…distracted me."

"You could finish now," he said. "Night school, online courses, whatever."

"I could," she said, and her tone suggested he shouldn't pursue the matter. "Do you have one? A college degree?"

"Bachelor's in Computer Engineering. UIUC."

"Sounds boring," she said, but with an undercurrent of envy. "In Chicago?"

"Urbana, but they have online courses too."

"So, if you studied tech stuff, how do you know so much about religion?"

"I read a lot. What was your degree going to be?"

"Sociology with a minor in criminal justice."

The oven timer buzzed. He didn't want to move, but Alyssa immediately sat up. "We don't have to hurry," he said. "They might need another five minutes."

"Or they might not," she said. "*You* set the timer, and we wouldn't want all your work to go to waste. Also, I'm *very* hungry." She was dressing, so he got up too.

The eggs were puffed and exactly brown enough, but he gave the muffins a little longer while he cut the eggs into squares and served the fruit, orange juice, and coffee.

"I could get very spoiled if I keep hanging out with you," she said.

"Good. I'd like to spoil you." He put out butter and jam for the muffins and checked them again. They looked perfect, and a toothpick in one came out clean. He was very pleased with how well everything had turned out, his Sunday offering for his beautiful Alyssa, and she *was* damned beautiful, no matter what she believed.

She was almost as pensive as she had been over the breakfast for supper after their first time, but whatever was on her mind didn't keep her from piling her plate with eggs, a generous helping of fruit, and two muffins slathered in butter.

Reid couldn't concentrate on the cheesy eggs or the crumbly sweetness of the muffins. He waited for her to speak, watching the way she licked a stray crumb from her lip, the way she held her fork.

Eventually she noticed. "What?" she asked.

"Nothing," he said.

She seemed uneasy, newly self-conscious, and sat a little straighter in her chair. "Tell me about Chicago," she suggested. "The Windy City, right?"

He had told her and Jane all the obvious things before and needed to think of something original to say. "It's not as windy as it sounds," he said. "Much taller buildings than here, and the wind off Lake Michigan, but you have sea breezes too."

"Near the coast on a good day," she agreed. "Do you miss the real weather?"

"It's not high on the list."

"Of things you miss? Do you want to go back?" The idea made her frown, a delicate little line forming between her eyebrows.

"Not at the moment," he said.

"Your dad is in Chicago?"

He nodded.

"Are you going back for Thanksgiving and Christmas?"

"I don't know."

"If you don't," she said, brightening a little, "you could cook Thanksgiving dinner for Jane and me…and your other friends, of course. I mean if you want to. Maybe you'd rather go out or be a guest."

"I like Jane," he said, "but…"

Alyssa put down her fork and took a sip of coffee. "We are not dating," she said. "We're friends. All three of us."

"Friends with benefits?"

"We are not doing that again."

"Okay," he said, and of course the word made her sigh in exasperation. She wanted him to stick up for himself, but he wasn't going to make demands like a jealous Neanderthal.

"I'm not saying it wasn't nice," she said grudgingly. "Especially, you know…when you took your time." She spoke matter-of-factly, but her cheeks were a little pink. "When nothing was in the oven," she clarified. "Even though I sort of ambushed you the first time. Last night…but it's not going to happen again."

"Can I kiss you?" he asked.

She raised an eyebrow. "Right now?"

"In general."

"Maybe. Maybe you should find somebody else. Jane is available, but maybe you'd prefer a nice unhappy wife."

"I gave wives up for Lent," he reminded her. In truth he had given them up when she filed for divorce.

"You were right," she said.

"I was? Why?"

"I love these eggs," she said. "You didn't tell me why they're Swiss, though."

"When I was little my mom always used Gruyère, which is more Swiss than so-called Swiss cheese, so that's probably why. "

"You miss her?"

"Yes."

"Me too. Nobody ever takes the place of your mother, not even if you live to be a hundred." She took a bite of muffin. "Yum," she said. "Tell me something cool about your mother."

He considered. "She used to celebrate little

holidays she invented just for us. Mustard Wednesday or National Oryx Day."

"What do you do on Mustard Wednesday?" she asked.

"Eat hot dogs, mostly."

"With all the fancy things you can cook, you eat hot dogs?"

"Hebrew National," he said. "French's classic yellow mustard. Potato salad made with Dijon and whole grain mustard. Even the coleslaw had mustard seed dressing in it."

"Oh," she said. "It's a serious religious holiday, then. When is it?"

"I think it was whenever she wanted it to be. On a Wednesday, of course."

"I would have liked your mom," she said.

"She would have liked you too."

"Am I making you sad?"

"Yup," he said matter-of-factly.

"Maybe we could do Mustard Wednesday sometime."

"Okay."

She shook her head. "I'm still waiting for you to show your true colors. I can't quite reconcile this laid-back, passive guy with somebody who pursues married women and ejects unwanted ex-husbands."

"I shouldn't have told you about the married women," he said. "Left my past in Chicago. My friend Noah said it was because I was afraid of commitment."

"Which works for me," she said. She brushed muffin crumbs from her fingers and got to her feet. She looked very proper and dignified in her long skirt, but he knew better.

"Don't rush off," he said, trying to sound casual.

"I have things to do before my shift," she said. "I'll be back on Tuesday—with Jane."

Chapter Eleven

On Tuesday, Reid left a message at the reception desk at Conavard to let them know he wouldn't be in the office for the next two days. It wasn't unusual, since he was sometimes at a work site all day, and he doubted anybody cared anyway. Patrick Heyerdahl was technically in charge, but in fact the company was in a state of limbo, waiting for Gloria Baird to decide whether to sell or reorganize. They all knew their jobs were on the line, and they did their best work without worrying about office niceties.

To ease his conscience, he worked right up until the doorbell rang. He had been working with difficult-to-read schematics and was wearing the reading glasses he almost never needed when he answered the door.

"Reid!" Jane cried. "How the hell are you?"

He looked for Alyssa, trying not to be obvious, and was relieved when she trailed in behind Jane. "I'm fine, Jane. How are you?"

"I'm good. Oh, you're so cute." She kissed him on the cheek. "You should wear those specs all the time."

He took them off. "I only need them for very small print." He looked beyond her and said, "Hello, Alyssa."

"Good morning, Four Eyes," she said.

"Don't be rude," Jane said cheerfully. They were both in blue jeans, straw hats, and sunglasses, but Alyssa wore a pretty, feminine blue blouse with smocking, and Jane a tight, unbuttoned three-button Henley, which made it clear she wasn't wearing a bra.

He found Alyssa's clothing far sexier—or maybe it was Alyssa, in anything at all. This was what was meant by *I only have eyes for you.* Jane is right, he thought. I'm a goner.

"Don't forget to put on sunscreen," Alyssa advised—not something he had been used to in Chicago in April.

Jane drove and insisted Reid sit beside her where he could see everything. After the school bus she drove every day, her Ford Excursion must have seemed like child's play, and she was a very skilled driver. Alyssa sat in the back seat and leaned forward to add her comments. Jane was an excellent tour guide, but he wished he could be alone with Alyssa, or at least sit where he could see her.

Jane offered a wealth of information on Carroll City history and took scenic drives to show off its natural assets. They made frequent stops to stroll on the beach or explore historic homes, gardens, a beautiful old lighthouse, and the ruins of a fort, which had once defended the shoreline. It was a lot of territory to cover in one day, and the ladies promised the second day would be more leisurely.

Reid was used to the beaches of Lake Michigan but had to admit the ocean was pretty spectacular. The salt air and hot sand had a summery scent that defied the season. Jane loved gift shops and accumulated a collection of souvenirs and presents for friends, while Alyssa was content to sit with Reid and watch the ocean. He was also impressed, not for the first time, by the abundance of eucalyptus trees and jacarandas, although he had yet to see anything like the fine old shade trees of Chicago neighborhoods.

Having made sure he wasn't prone to seasickness, they also took him out on a whale-watching boat. It was late in the season, and they didn't see much, but the ride was fun anyway. The highlight for him was watching Alyssa's hair blow in the wind while she laughed and held onto her hat.

Lunch was hot, juicy burgers on the beach, but for dinner they took him to their favorite restaurant, where they assured him the Mexican cuisine was more authentic than anything he could have had in Chicago. The setting was certainly atmospheric, with colorful umbrellas shading tables in a hacienda courtyard and strolling mariachis to serenade them. The ladies insisted on ordering Quique's world-famous strawberry margaritas, which at least meant Alyssa no longer believed he might be an alcoholic.

While he perused the menu, Jane quizzed him about his own recipes. "Can you make enchiladas? What do you put in your tacos?"

The margaritas were indeed excellent, and Jane didn't drink enough of hers to cause concern about her driving. They gave him conflicting advice about what to order, and in the end, he ignored them both and chose the tequila lime salmon. Alyssa ordered tamales, and Jane chicken chimichanga, "because I like to say it."

"Do you remember the night we met?" Reid asked Alyssa. "You said you didn't want to go out to dinner with me, with or without Jane."

"Do you blame me?" she asked.

"No, but I'm glad you changed your mind."

"I like it best when you cook," Jane said.

"Good," he said. "There are so many things I'd like to cook for you."

"Like what?" she asked eagerly.

He gave her a few examples, but in truth he could not have matched Quique's tequila lime salmon. The fish was tender and moist, and the sauce creamy and perfectly seasoned. The dish was further enhanced by the congenial company.

They were adamant that he was their guest and should not be allowed to pay for anything, but finally consented to let him leave the tip, which he made a generous one. The pretty Latina waitress had given them excellent service, but she was not the one he was trying to impress.

****

On Wednesday, he had barely finished a quick breakfast of bulgur porridge with apricots and almonds when the doorbell rang. It was Alyssa, in blue jeans, a plain green T-shirt, and a short brown jacket. He had thought the teal dress she wore to go dancing was the perfect color for her, but now he wondered if there was any shade she couldn't wear well.

"Good morning," he said.

She didn't respond, coming in without a word. She looked grumpy. And she was alone. "Is something wrong?" he asked.

"Jane has a sore throat," she said.

He tried not to be glad. "I'm sorry," he said quickly. "Will she be okay?"

"She might be contagious," Alyssa said as if it were a character failing, "or she might be setting us up, but if she *is* sick, would you make her some bean soup

120

like you did for me?"

"Sure," he said. "I'd be glad to."

"Have you had your flu shot?" she asked.

"Yes. Do you want to cancel?"

"No," she said, "but we would have more fun with Jane. Jane is fun. She also has a better car."

"You can drive my Malibu," he offered.

"Oh, like 'Baby, you can drive my car'?"

"Are you going to be like this all day?" he asked.

"Maybe," she said. She put her hands in her pockets. "Let's go."

Her foul mood continued as they explored the Carroll City Zoo. "We'll just hit a few highlights," she said, "because you can spend a whole day here easily." Reid admired the elaborate, well-maintained animal enclosures and the lovely spring weather, and all she had to say was, "Rug rats everywhere."

She softened a bit as they watched a toddler engage with a young orangutan through the glass. They were fascinated with one another, matching gestures and expressions, the little boy addressing his new friend as "grilla." The child's mother didn't correct him, and an increasing number of bystanders snapped pictures with their cameras and cell phones. Reid and Alyssa stood back a little, and she slipped her cool hand into his. "Cute," she said as they strolled on.

"So, you do like children?" he asked.

"Of course," she said.

No glass, only a deep trench, separated the path from the enclosure where the massive hippos stood stolidly in the water. They were too ugly and smelly to be entertaining, but Alyssa was amused by a young man who kept urging the preteen girl with him to "look at the hipotamus." She smiled, and it was like the sun coming out after rain, like a beautiful arching rainbow. The day became immediately more enjoyable.

"Do you think that's okay?" he asked, gesturing toward the girl. "Guy alone with a girl so young?"

She gave them a disinterested glance. "They're siblings or cousins or something," she said. "Don't you see the resemblance?"

He didn't. "No. I guess that's why you're the police officer," he said.

"Does it bother you? Me being a cop?"

"No, why would it?"

"Some guys don't like it." She lowered her voice to growl, "This is a man's world, baby."

"I can see why they might be threatened," he acknowledged, "but no…I'm impressed that you do such a difficult job."

"I'm a street cop, not some hotshot detective."

"But you go into places most people would run from. Every time you go out on a call, you don't know what the situation will develop into. I couldn't do it, and I'm amazed that you can, but it certainly hasn't made you unfeminine."

"Jane said you swore when she told you what I do."

"Only because I woke you up to bail me out. I knew you thought I was a terrible person, anyway."

"Yeah, I did," she said. She gave him a playful shove. "I still do."

Another highlight was an enclosure shared by swamp monkeys and otters and equipped with rocks for climbing and a waterfall. A monkey and an otter competed for one of the flat boulders in a pool where the otter had been sunning. They batted at one another and grabbed tails, the loser of each skirmish sliding into the water, only to come back for another try. Alyssa leaned over the rail to watch. "In all the times I've been here, I've never seen them interact this way," she said. "The monkeys play and fight all the time, but this is the first time I've seen one interact with an otter."

"I didn't know they could climb," Reid said as another otter flopped onto a high rock and slid down the waterfall.

"Do they have otters in the Chicago zoo?" she asked.

"Yes, in Brookfield and Lincoln Park both, and Lincoln Park is free. I must admit yours is very impressive, though."

"We like it," Alyssa said smugly.

They ate lunch at a patio table on a shaded terrace. Reid would have liked to take Alyssa to one of the zoo's fancier restaurants and buy her a lavish meal, but she still insisted she and Jane were paying for everything, and she favored the open-air ambience of what was basically a fast-food place. He had to agree it was pleasant—just enough shade, just enough breeze, and the soft fragrance of trees heavy with tropical flowers. She asked what he wanted to drink—they offered soft drinks, bottled water, and tea, and cartons of milk—but not what he would like to eat. She sent him to claim a table while she ordered and paid for the food.

She came out on the terrace with a tray loaded with hot dogs, French fries, small plastic tubs of potato salad, and bottles of tea with lemon. He stood to take it from her, which she seemed to appreciate. "I'll be right back," she said, and she was, with napkins and plastic forks. She opened her purse and dumped a few packets of catsup for the French fries and at least twenty mustard packets onto the tray. "Today is Mustard Wednesday," she explained. "I asked if the potato salad had mustard in it, but they didn't know. Maybe you can tell."

"I think it's more or less standard," he said. He tried to sound casual, but her gesture had touched something deep inside. He covered by taking a forkful of potato salad. "Yes," he said. "Yellow mustard. Thank you." He wanted to lean across the table and kiss her, but she hadn't answered his query about whether kissing was to be permissible in this relationship. What had she said? Maybe?

The hot dogs were not top quality, but they were hot enough and tasted pretty good slathered with mustard. There was plenty of mustard for the hot, salty French fries too, which was a new taste experience. The important thing was that she had done this for him and was transparently pleased with herself. Reid was quite happy enjoying the food and the sunshine in her company, until he kept noticing the same figure about twenty feet away.

The guy was in front of a large parrot cage, but he wasn't watching the birds. He was swarthy, tough-looking, medium height, maybe thirty-five, with slicked-back dark hair. He was dressed all in black—cargo pants, boots, and a T-shirt with rolled sleeves. He was fit and muscular, with an indistinct tattoo on his right bicep. He looked capable of bashing in somebody's head with a tire iron.

"Alyssa," Reid said. "Don't look now, but the guy

over by the cage to your left? I think he's watching us."
He expected her, being a police officer, to know how to
scope the guy out without being obvious, but instead
she did what most people would do when told not to
look—she looked. She looked long and hard, and the
man in black ducked his head and slunk away.

"You often have that effect on people?" he asked.

"It's my superpower. How come it doesn't work on
you?" She smiled and bit into a French fry. "I shouldn't
eat any more of these," she said, and helped herself to
another one.

He had forgotten she'd given them up for Lent and
wasn't going to remind her now. He was still unnerved,
not least by Alyssa's cool handling of another poor slob
attracted by her lovely face. "I think I need to tell you
something," he said.

"Oh, oh, sounds serious," she said. She spoke
lightly, as if she was joking, but the little line between
her eyebrows was back.

He took a deep breath. "The reason Detective
Macias doesn't think I'm a suspect anymore is that he
thinks I was the intended target. He thinks somebody
meant to kill *me*."

She stared at him for about thirty seconds. "You're
joking…right?"

"No."

"Or making a play to get sympathy?"

"No, but I wouldn't mind a little about now. So far
all I'm getting is paranoid."

"Why would anybody want to kill *you*?"

"I have no idea."

She considered. "Did you like invent some super
code somebody would want to steal?"

He had to laugh. "No. Maybe Baird did, though. The killer may have sat at his desk—he left fingerprints. I don't know what it's about, but Macias...I can't believe he didn't tell you, or isn't there a police grapevine or something?"

She shrugged.

"Maybe I shouldn't be surprised," he said. "I don't think he has a lot of respect for you or for women in general."

"Macias? Yeah, he's a turd," Alyssa agreed. "I don't exactly hobnob with the detectives, you know." She took a deep breath and pushed away her half-empty potato salad container. "Make sure all your windows are locked," she said. "Don't just look—try to open them. If the killer is somebody who was at the housewarming or in your apartment for any reason, he could have tampered with them. Make sure you know who's at the door before you unlock it. Don't automatically open up like you did this morning. Use the chain." She frowned. "The weakest point of entry in your place is the sliding door to the balcony. The lock isn't worth shit, and don't think you're safe because you're on the fifth floor. Put in a security bar."

"Thank you, Officer," he said. "I thought I was safe there until this minute. Baird was killed at work, and I sort of assumed the killer wouldn't know where I lived."

"You're welcome," she said. "All part of the service. Seriously, be careful. Jane wouldn't like it if her favorite cook got whacked." She munched on a French fry and then said more seriously, "I should tell you something too."

"Okay."

"I need to apologize to you…for leading you on."

"What? No…"

"I shouldn't have done what I did and let you think it would go on. I started it, and you had a right to expect it to continue, and I can't. I don't know what I was thinking, but I didn't mean to hurt you."

"It's okay," he said.

"No, it isn't. I'm sorry." She studied him, her eyes soft with concern.

"It's okay," he repeated.

"You're not mad?"

"No, Alyssa, I'm not mad. Let's just enjoy today. After all, it's Mustard Wednesday." He smiled at her and picked up a packet to make his point.

****

After lunch they drove to nearby Carroll Park. The place was truly impressive, a combination of open space and cultural attractions with stunning Spanish colonial architecture and a view of distant mountains under the clear blue sky. "Why is everything named Carroll?" Reid asked.

"They were a founding family and major philanthropists," Alyssa explained. "This land used to belong to them, and they gave it to the city to build all this. There are about a dozen museums," she said. "Where would you like to start?"

"Whatever you like best," he said.

They visited five museums, which was enough for one day. What Reid enjoyed most was learning about Alyssa's tastes by observing what she lingered in front of and what merited barely a glance. In the Museum of Art, he learned how much she liked color and detail, regardless of the style or subject. Both abstract and realistic works held her attention.

"What is it supposed to be?" he asked of one painting she stopped to study.

"I don't know," she said, "but I like it." The placard beside it might have explained the meaning, but neither of them bothered to read it.

She also liked California history, he discovered, fossils, black-and-white photography, and the massive cars of the thirties and forties. He liked everything she liked and could no longer tell what he would have preferred on his own. If she was happy, he was happy.

After Carroll Park, the last stop of the day was a storefront housing the Police Museum, dedicated to the history of the CCPD. Alyssa knew the volunteer on duty, a retired female officer, and Reid showed his support by purchasing his only souvenir of the day, a black T-shirt with the CCPD logo. It bore a distinct resemblance to a Soviet Olympics uniform, but the association with Alyssa was irresistible. She was particularly interested in showing him the exhibits relating to the role of women in the department. In front of the display of the uniform of the first policewomen, circa 1900, he said, "You would look very cute in this getup."

"One thing I've never been is *cute,*" she said scornfully. "Cops are not cute."

Other attractions included a crossing guard badge from her elementary school and the video of a lengthy downtown standoff vividly remembered from her childhood—her father had been in the thick of the action and helped take down the gunman.

****

Jane had been left on her own for lunch, and

Alyssa wanted to get back before she had to make dinner as well. He needed very little persuasion to get her to stop at the Italian market to buy the makings of a sickroom-friendly supper. "She needs protein and flavonoids," he said, "and we should avoid dairy." If Jane was too ill for company, he would make her some soup and take the bus home.

Jane looked miserable enough to make Alyssa feel guilty about suspecting her of malingering, but she was up for company. She wore a long flannel robe and no makeup and was flushed and droopy-eyed.

"Hell of a note for your spring break," Reid told her and happily set about cooking bean soup and making turkey-and-cranberry sandwiches, a spinach-and-grapefruit salad, and tea with honey and lemon, while Alyssa sat at the table and rehashed the day's activities for Jane. She didn't mention his paranoia at the zoo.

"What kind of bread is this?" Jane asked when he set the plates of food in front of them. "It looks all weird."

"Eat it," Alyssa advised. "It's good for you."

"It's Italian multigrain bread," he said. "If it scratches your throat, just eat the turkey. It will help boost your immune system."

Jane took a bite of the sandwich. "How come you're so smart?" she asked.

"I don't feel very smart," he said, "but you're good for my ego."

She took another bite. "This is very good," she admitted.

Jane shuffled back to bed right after supper, and Reid loaded the dishwasher. He didn't think he should linger and planned to take the next bus, but Alyssa insisted on driving him home. "This is a full-service door-to-door tour," she said.

She parked in the garage and got out of the car. "Are you coming up?" he asked, pleased but surprised.

"Don't get any ideas," she said. "I'm just going to do a security check."

"So, you don't think I'm paranoid?"

"Oh, I'm sure you are," she said, "but just because you're paranoid doesn't mean nobody's out to get you."

In the apartment, she examined the door chain, checked all the windows, and looked in the shower and the closets. "Aren't you going to check under the bed?" he asked.

"Don't be cute," she said. She strode out on the balcony to look around before she locked the sliding door. "Buy a security bar tomorrow," she said. "Get a good one. Try the hardware store downtown—Jackson Street near Tenth. They'll give you good advice."

"Baird was killed months ago," he said. "If somebody was after me, wouldn't he have done it by now?"

"Maybe," she said, "or maybe he's waiting for things to calm down or for you to get careless. Don't oblige him." Her job done, she returned to the living room.

"Thank you," he said. "For the excellent tour and the security consultation. Thank Jane again for me too."

"You were very well brought up," she said.

They had been together all day, and he didn't like letting her go. At the door he kissed her goodbye and was surprised by her response. She met him more than halfway, her lips soft and willing. The scent of her hair and her subtle perfume filled his head with a dizzy sweetness. She had drawn a line—did she want him to cross it? Better not—such assumptions could be dangerous. Knowing what making love with her was like and being denied it was hard, but the longing he had for her now had nothing to do with the way their bodies fit together. What surprised him was the matching hunger he sensed in her. He almost asked her to stay, but while he hesitated, she said, "Good night," and then she was gone.

He had felt safe enough in the apartment before Alyssa's police-trained response, but now he was a little on edge. He was determined to put the threat out of his mind and return to business as usual, but before he went to bed, he put a coat hanger in the track of the sliding door to the balcony. It could still be forced open but might make enough noise to alert him.

He thought about Alyssa and the day they had spent together before he finally fell asleep, but the anonymous threat haunted his dreams. A man all in black, like the one at the zoo, entered the apartment, not through the balcony door, but by breaking through the front door. He had a machine gun and inexplicably wore a gas mask. Reid sat up, gasping for air and certain he smelled smoke. He got out of bed and checked all the doors and windows again, turned on all the lights, and repeated Alyssa's search of possible hiding places.

He didn't think he would go back to sleep, but he did. This time the intruder wore a beret and the kind of overcoat he hadn't seen since he left Chicago. Reid didn't see a weapon, but as the stranger approached the bed, he knew he was about to die. He couldn't move to defend himself—he was completely paralyzed. He tried to yell, but no sound would come, and finally the effort woke him.

Chapter Twelve

In the morning light Reid felt foolish. Nobody was trying to kill him. It was all some colossal joke, and he would be ungrateful if he let Alyssa's gesture of concern make him feel less, instead of more, secure.

He stayed aware of his surroundings all day, checking out every rider who boarded the bus on the way to and from Conavard, but the mundane details of the office had a calming effect. Surprisingly, the source of the problem, the site of Baird's murder, now struck him as too normal to be unsafe. When his mind wandered from his work, he didn't think of violence. He thought about kissing Alyssa.

He had lunch at his desk, a mediocre ham-and-cheese sandwich from the deli downstairs, and while he was eating, Goff stuck his head in the door and asked if Detective Macias had asked him any more questions.

"No, not lately."

"Hm," was all Goff said in reply.

"Why?" Reid asked.

Goff shrugged and disappeared.

****

Alyssa called in the evening, not long after he got home. "Sunday is Easter," she said. "Go to church with me?"

"I'd love to," he said without hesitation. "Brunch afterward?"

"I don't…"

"Hot cross buns for Easter, right? Crisp bacon, maybe pancakes? Whatever you'd like."

"I don't think I should go to your apartment again."

"I'll be good," he promised.

"Yes, but will I? You could come to our place. Jane isn't too sick to enjoy the company, and she likes to watch you cook."

He didn't want Jane, sick or not, to watch him cook. "I have a better kitchen," he said. She maintained a stubborn silence, so he said, "You should ask her what she wants. She might not feel up to it. We don't have to decide right now."

"Fine," she said stiffly. "I'll pick you up at eight."

He felt bad after he hung up, depressed. Maybe it wasn't going to work for them to be friends. Was it enough to be around her, to hear her voice? Was it better than nothing, or did he need to make a clean break?

****

Friday morning, Detective Macias called him at Conavard, the first time they had spoken without Reid being summoned to an interrogation room. "Do you know Neal Trayner?" he asked without preamble, but at least his tone was polite.

"Yes," Reid answered.

"He wasn't on your list," Macias pointed out.

"Sorry. He's the guy who delivers the office mail. I'm not sure I knew his name yet when I made the list."

"You've become…more friendly recently?"

"No, I've barely spoken to him. Why? He can't be a suspect."

"Why is that?"

"Have you seen him? He looks about seventeen and lives with his mother."

"Trust me, appearances can be deceiving," Macias assured him.

Reid didn't think Neal could have wielded the tire iron with enough force to kill Baird, but the possibility that he was the person who wanted him dead was almost comforting. He couldn't be in much danger from such a source. Neal had acne, bit his fingernails, and was passionately devoted to Taylor Swift.

"Anyway," Macias said, "you might be interested in the story he had to tell."

"What story?" Reid leaned back in his chair. If the detective was going to waste his time, he could at least be comfortable.

"Mr. Trayner claims Mr. Baird took him out for a drink not long after he started working in the building. He'd found out it was his birthday, his twenty-first. He took him to the Monkey Wrench cocktail lounge. He says Baird insisted he try a particular mixed drink, and later he suspected he had put something in his glass. He said he was more hung over than he could explain. Of course, by the looks of this kid, it wouldn't take much alcohol to put him in a coma. He further states Baird came on to him, propositioned him, although he wasn't sure at first what he meant. He said no and left right away and was smart enough to take a cab home."

"Oh my God," Reid said and guiltily remembered Alyssa, who didn't seem to mind any other profanity.

"Shall we go over your story about drinking with Baird again?" Macias asked. "Anything you'd like to add?"

"No, I told you everything. As much as I could

remember anyway. But…if he put something in my drink, would it be grounds to clear the DUI charge?"

"They would have had to do a tox screen to prove it. And it wouldn't change your BA—you consumed the alcohol voluntarily. You could have knowingly taken the drug too." He was right, but the possibility still made Reid feel better. "Are you sure he didn't try anything? Hint at anything?"

"If he did, I was oblivious. So…what do you think? This skinny kid who delivers the mail took offense at Baird's clumsy seduction attempt and bashed his head in? If he had, he wouldn't hand you the motive, would he?"

"Stranger things have happened," Macias said. "But no, I don't like him for it. He wasn't the person who left fingerprints in the office anyway. There may be an innocent explanation for the prints, of course—a cleaning lady we overlooked or some such. Sitting in a dead guy's chair isn't a crime. Somebody else may have had the same motive, though—for Baird. Damned if I can figure out what it has to do with you…unless he was using your name—but then there's the picture. It's a puzzle, and some of the pieces are still missing."

Reid would have liked to speculate further, but the conversation was abruptly terminated when the detective had to take another call. He was surprised he wanted to go on talking to Macias. He didn't like the man, but he had access to the most information on the case at his fingertips. Reluctantly he put the matter out of his mind and turned back to his computer screen.

Chapter Thirteen

Alyssa must have felt bad too, because when she picked Reid up Sunday morning, she said, "I was afraid you would cancel because I was sort of mean on the phone." She wore the same outfit as the previous week, with the addition of a gold cross on a chain around her neck. She also had a scarf over her hair, although he understood head coverings were no longer required and Easter bonnets now unfashionable.

"Mean? No, you weren't mean. How is Jane feeling today?"

She sighed. "She was still in bed when I left. She's—not cranky, she never is, but tired of being sick. You know. I hope I don't get it."

"She probably won't want company," he said, trying not to sound hopeful.

"I don't know," Alyssa said. She kept her tone neutral.

"This is a discussion for later," he said. "Right now, we're going to church." He opened the door, and she went out ahead of him. Standing in front of the elevator, he said, "I don't think I've been to an Easter mass before. Anything I should know?"

She studied him gravely and said, "I don't know what you believe."

"That's okay," he said. "Neither do I."

They were in the garage and she had started the car

before she spoke again. "My faith is important to me," she said.

"I know. You're lucky. Not everybody can get there."

"Most people think religion is stupid," she said.

"What people?" he asked. "Other cops?"

"Yes," she said. "And Jane…"

"Yes, and look at her life. Where is she headed?"

"I like Jane," she said.

"So do I, but I wouldn't want to marry her."

"Who asked you to?" she said scornfully. "You don't want to marry anybody. The world is full of other men's wives."

"Okay," he said. He didn't want to argue and sat in silence, staring out the window. He glanced in the rearview mirror to be sure they weren't being followed, knowing his paranoia was ridiculous.

"I'm sorry," she said. "That was mean too."

"Maybe it was never about cheating or fear of commitment. Maybe I was attracted to women who were filling that role because it was what I wanted for myself…a wife."

"Yeah," she said, "barefoot and pregnant and chained to the kitchen stove. Or maybe you'd rather do the cooking yourself, but if a subservient wife is what you want—"

"I like it that you're strong and independent," he protested. "All the women I've ever loved have been strong individuals with careers of their own."

"You may be attracted to those women, but that doesn't mean you'll want to live with one," she said.

"Are you talking about me or Knight?" She had nothing to say in reply, and after a minute, he said, "I'm sorry. I don't want to fight."

"Do you believe in God?" she asked abruptly.

"I don't know," he said. "Does God believe in me?"

She gave him a quick, worried glance, as if she wasn't sure whether he was being flippant or not. "Yes, He does," she said. "So, you're an agnostic."

"If you need a label."

"Do you know about Pascal's wager?" she asked.

"Yes. It's a cop-out. Faith is faith, not a gamble."

"So…you take religion seriously," she said. She sounded surprised and impressed.

He decided the wisest thing to say was nothing.

She changed the subject. "Did you get the bar for the balcony door?"

"Yes. I always follow the advice of my security consultant."

****

St. Anthony's was decorated for Easter with lilies and other flowers at the altar, mixing an aroma of spring with its air of holiness. Lengths of white ribbon were looped at the end of each pew. Attendance was far better than it had been the previous week. Alyssa again found them a seat about halfway back, on the aisle this time. Everybody was dressed in their finest, and more than a few of the older women wore hats or lace chapel veils. They were early, and people continued to enter as they sat waiting.

Alyssa was explaining the Paschal vigil, which had ended at sunrise, when an older man in a sober, dark suit stopped to speak to her. Reid knew who he was before she said, "This is my father, Captain Sharpe. Dad, my friend Reid Lucas."

Sharpe gave him a look of open disapproval reminiscent of Paul Knight. "Mr. Lucas," he said stiffly.

"Captain Sharpe. I'm very glad to meet you," Reid said. He offered his hand, hoping the man would at least be civil in church on Easter Sunday. Above all, he didn't want Alyssa to be embarrassed.

Sharpe shook hands, his grip almost painfully firm, but didn't return the sentiment. "Your mother missed you on Wednesday," he told his daughter sternly.

She didn't mention that her mother probably wouldn't have known who she was. "I dropped by Friday night," she said, a shade defensive. "You were out. Didn't Meg tell you?"

"She might have mentioned it." He had nothing more to say and left to find a seat somewhere behind them.

"You were supposed to see your mother on Wednesday and spent the day with me instead?" Reid asked.

"Don't *you* start," she said.

The Easter mass was very impressive, solemn and moving, and the sermon full of the joy of resurrection and the promise of spring. It might have more spiritual meaning to Alyssa, but he was sure he was as glad to be here as she was, to sit and stand and kneel beside her, although he didn't know why she had asked him to come. To show her father she had moved on, even if she hadn't?

As they filed out of the church afterward, she spoke briefly to several people and stopped longer to talk to others, apparently people she hadn't seen in a while. She introduced him to the latter group, always as her friend. She gave no further explanation, and they asked for none. On the steps she was approached by two dark-haired men who were very glad to see her. One of them hugged her, and the other, tall and handsome, told her how nice she looked. "This is my friend, Reid Lucas," she told them, and to Reid, "Frank Nichols and Kurt Bond. We met in high school drama class. They're both wonderful actors."

"She's exaggerating," Kurt said. "We dabble in community theater, but we have very boring day jobs." He offered a firm handshake and a friendly smile. He was much better-looking and clearly nicer than Paul Knight, and Reid envied how well they both seemed to know Alyssa.

"So does he," she said. "Computer software."

"Someone has to do it," Frank said. He smiled too but didn't shake hands.

"We can't all be as macho as you," Kurt agreed.

"Nice to see you, sweetheart," Frank said warmly to Alyssa.

After they left, Reid asked, "Was he your old boyfriend?"

"Which one?" She was visibly amused. "They're a couple."

"Really?"

"They're getting married this summer. They don't all fit the stereotypes, you know."

"You met in drama class? Did you want to be an actress?"

"No, I wanted an easy elective. And the cutest boys took drama—I was never into the football player type."

"Good," he said. He took her hand, and she didn't object. "I played hockey."

****

141

Jane was up when they got to the apartment, slouched on the couch in front of the television set in her robe and slippers. She was watching an animated feature with an Easter theme and looked better than she had on Wednesday. "Hey, Reid," she said. "Are you all holy now?"

"Hi, Jane."

"What are you going to cook for us?"

"I don't know," he said. "What do you have for me to work with?"

"You don't have to," Alyssa said. She took off her scarf and tucked it in her skirt pocket.

"Somebody has to cook something," Jane said. "I'm starving."

"I'll take a look," he said and headed for the kitchen. Pancakes would be easy if they had a few staples. If they didn't, the Italian market probably wasn't open on Easter Sunday.

"I'm sorry," Alyssa said behind him. "I know it would be easier in your kitchen."

"This will be fine," he said. "Do you mind?" He gestured toward the cupboards, asking permission to make free with her kitchen. He opened a few doors, relieved to see somebody had been shopping recently. The refrigerator was even more promising. Jane came in too and sat at the table to supervise. At least she didn't have the energy to get underfoot.

He made pancakes and fried bacon, thinking of the lavish menu he might have planned if he'd been able to do the occasion justice. Vanilla crepes, pumpkin caramel French toast, bagels with yogurt and smoked salmon, ham and spinach omelet, steel cut oatmeal with raisins and honey…

At least everything turned out well, the bacon lean and crisp and the pancakes thick and fluffy, with walnuts added for crunch. Their syrup was cheap, low-calorie stuff and past its expiration date, so he made his own topping with yogurt, vanilla, and honey. They had plenty of orange juice and coffee, and Alyssa made lemon ginger tea for the convalescent.

"So, are you Catholic now?" Jane asked, loading her plate. Her illness obviously hadn't affected her appetite.

"No," he said. "It's not contagious."

"He's very spiritual, though," Alyssa said.

Jane rolled her eyes.

"Are we back to talking about me in the third person?" Reid asked.

"He's getting feisty," Jane said approvingly.

"Why *did* you ask me to go to church with you?" he asked Alyssa.

Put on the spot, she took a bite of pancake, her soft, sensitive lips caressing the fork. "Because," she said, as if that was answer enough, and then, with a little shrug, "I wanted to. Reid, these are the best pancakes I've ever tasted."

"Mm-hm," Jane agreed.

"Thank you," he said, but they were just pancakes. He wanted to lay a feast of ambrosia before Alyssa, to seduce her with flavors and textures she'd never encountered before. Yes, he was definitely done for.

"How do you get the bacon so crisp and even?" Jane asked. "It's never like this in restaurants."

"Constant attention," he said. "Restaurants don't have the time."

"Uh-huh," she said dubiously. "The frying pan's

not what you were paying attention to." She twitched her eyebrows in a Groucho Marx leer.

Alyssa gave her a sharp look and turned her gaze accusingly on Reid.

"You're imagining things," he said, and to change the subject asked, "Are you going to be able to go back to work tomorrow, Jane?"

"Oh sure. I couldn't do *her* job," she said, gesturing toward Alyssa, "but driving little monsters around, yeah."

"Are you working today?" he asked Alyssa, meaning *How long can I stretch this visit?*

"Four-to-midnight shift," she said.

"Please be careful," he said. "The streets are dangerous after dark."

"The streets are always dangerous," she said. "Yesterday…" She waved a dismissive hand. "But I got to see a baby born. Very cool. And do you know what the most dangerous thing on the streets is, to cops and citizens? Drunk and distracted drivers."

"We did not get off to the best start," he acknowledged. "But I swear to you I will never again get behind the wheel when I've had even a taste of alcohol. Lesson learned."

Jane ate voraciously, cleaned her plate, and then said, "I think I need to take a nap. Rest up for tomorrow." She rose, started to lean toward Reid to kiss his cheek, and stopped when she remembered her germs. "I'll see you guys later. Happy Easter." She said it as if she was joking.

After she was gone, Alyssa kept her gaze on her plate, chasing a stray bite of pancake.

"Is she okay?" he asked.

She looked up. "Yes," she said, and he guessed, from her mutinous expression, that she believed Jane had set them up. "She thinks I should be dating," she said.

"That's not for her to decide."

"No, it isn't. I'm not ready, but she thinks I should be. And she thinks it might as well be you."

"Because I'm harmless?" he guessed.

Alyssa exhaled, exasperated. "You are not harmless," she said.

He studied her, trying to understand what she was thinking, to get past his own feelings. "You know I would never hurt you," he said.

"Not on purpose anyway." She took a last morsel of bacon. "Even cocker spaniel puppies sometimes bite." She pushed her plate away and got up, ready to clear the table.

"Let me," he said. "I'll load the dishwasher, since you'll have to unload it."

She continued to gather plates. "I don't like the way you do it," she objected, reclaiming the kitchen as her territory.

"Tell me how you want it done, then," he said reasonably. He reached for her silverware, and their hands touched briefly.

She pretended she didn't notice. "Some handles up and some down," she said.

"Okay." It sounded reasonable to him, but he always put them all down. "I understand loading the dishwasher is a primary source of domestic discord, right up there with sex, money, and leaving the toilet seat up."

"We can do better than that," she said.

He was still trying to figure out what she meant when she closed and started the dishwasher and turned away. He was standing too close, and they all but collided. Reid couldn't resist the opportunity, the scent of her hair enticingly near. He kissed her.

She held him off a little at first, but soon yielded and relaxed into it, soft and vulnerable. She looked like an innocent young girl in her navy blouse and the gold cross around her neck, but he could feel every part of her body against his, as if for the first time…or the last?

He wanted her so much, in every way, not merely the physical, although touching her would be the expression of everything else he felt.

She was enjoying the moment as much as he was, so he kept kissing her, nuzzled her neck, gently touched her breast, and then she pushed him away. "Don't," she said, but she didn't seem angry. "I don't want to do this."

"Then we won't," he said. He took a deep breath, holding onto his self-control.

"I'm sorry," she said.

"Don't be. I'm good at this."

"What?"

"Denial. Married women…"

"Is that what you like?" she asked. "Your little fantasy? 'No, please, I can't, my husband will find out'?"

"I don't think…"

"I'm sorry. That was an awful thing to say."

"It's okay."

"Anyway, I'm not married anymore," she reminded him.

"Maybe you are. It's not always easy to let go and

move on."

"I want to, though. Move on."

"I know. You will…Maybe I should go."

She hesitated before she nodded, as if she was reluctant to see him go…or was he indulging in wishful thinking? "I'll drive you home," she said. "The buses will be on the holiday schedule."

Making a clean break would be easier right now, but how could he resist the opportunity to spend a few more minutes in her presence?

****

They didn't talk much in the car. At the last minute, as she pulled into the empty parking spot next to his, he said, "I love you."

"Don't say that," she protested. "I love you too," she added, but her tone suggested she was already taking it back, as if the words were meaningless.

He leaned over to give her a quick, deliberately impersonal kiss and got out of the car. He glanced around the garage and saw nothing out of the ordinary—fewer cars than was usual on the weekend, as was to be expected at this hour on Easter Sunday—but thoughts of Alyssa crowded out even his paranoia. Could there be any more insincere line in the English language than *I love you too?*

The garage, dim even this time of day, was suddenly filled with light and sound. Headlights swerved toward him from beyond the elevator. In a hundred movies and TV shows this scene played out with the threatened character running straight ahead of the onrushing vehicle. He knew better and found himself doing the same thing. Almost too late he veered away and slammed into a parked car, feeling the shock of pain through his hip and ribs.

The pursuer veered too and hit the parked car near the right taillight. Someone was making a serious effort to kill him. The knowledge came with a jolt as physical as pain. Baird's killer was trying to add him to the list *right now.* He bounced off the parked car and scrambled desperately toward the hood and the narrow space between it and the wall, until he realized the assailant had only to ram into the back and crush him.

Where was safety? In his car? The elevator? Outside to the street where the killer might hesitate to run him down in front of witnesses—if there were any? For all his focus on Alyssa, he had no sense of whether she was still nearby.

With a squeal of tires, the vehicle—a dark, late-model SUV—reversed as if to take another shot at him, and Reid ran again. If more residents had been home, he could have stayed between the cars, but too many people were out to church or brunch or family events, and he found himself exposed. The SUV charged straight at him. He almost dodged out of the way, but the bumper slammed into him and threw him against the wall. His head hit the concrete, and everything faded to black.

Chapter Fourteen

Reid woke up slumped against the wall, his head aching, and opened his eyes to see a man leaning over him. When he realized Reid was awake, he said, "Shit." Reid recognized neither the face nor the voice, but the wavy blond hair was familiar. The man who had groped Jane in the elevator was here in the garage, no longer elegant, dressed in black jeans and a black turtleneck, and Reid must have been dreaming again or hallucinating, because it all made about as much sense as the beret or the gas mask in his nightmares.

He could see two vehicles beyond the man's dark shape. The SUV hadn't been able to back up again because a white car blocked the way, and the driver's door stood open. The man behind the wheel had had to get out to finish him off. Reid saw everything with perfect clarity, but he knew he was asleep. It was what they called lucid dreaming, and all he had to do was wake up.

"You're dead, motherfucker," the blond man said and lifted his arm. He had a knife, not a tire iron, a long, narrow, fixed blade, and Reid's fuzzy brain finally registered the white car as Alyssa's, and he knew he had to fight back, because he could die, and it might be what he deserved, but the possibility of Alyssa being hurt was intolerable.

The knife couldn't be real either because the hand

wrapped around the hilt was bent back at the wrist at a very odd angle. The weapon fell and clattered on the floor. The blond man gave an undignified yelp, twisted away from Reid, stumbled, and fell to his knees. A second later he was flat on the concrete, face against the floor, with a navy-clad knee on his spine.

For the second time in their short acquaintance, Alyssa Knight appeared to Reid as an angel of mercy, rescuing him from the unthinkable. She wound a piece of cloth—her scarf?—around the big man's wrists and knotted it with more than necessary force and then stood and kicked the knife aside. The perp struggled and tried to roll over, and she put a foot in the small of his back. It didn't have as high a heel as Jane's, but it took the fight out of him. He didn't say anything beyond a few muttered curses.

"My purse is in the car," Alyssa said calmly. "Do you have your cell phone?" Reid still felt the paralysis of a dream, and he struggled to slip his hand into his pocket. "Call 911," she said, and then she looked at him with more annoyance than concern. "The year isn't half gone," she said, "and I've had more action than in the previous three. You're some kind of a jinx."

He dragged out his phone and got slowly to his feet. His head hurt, and there was a deep ache in his ribs, but he was alive, and he was awake, and this was all real, all of it. His fingers were clumsy on the phone, and he held it out to her. She took it with a sigh, and as she punched in the numbers, she said, "At least I didn't have to fire my gun. The shooting review board is a real headache."

"Alyssa," he said faintly.

"Yeah? Are you okay? You hit your head? Did you

lose consciousness?" Before he could answer, she turned away and spoke briskly into the phone. How could he feel as if he meant nothing to her when she had just saved his life?

Not until after the squad car arrived with its flashing lights and Alyssa, still in her skirt and heels with the cross around her neck, had helped put the assailant in the back seat and conferred with her colleagues did she come and put her arms around him. They clung together for dear life, and he could feel how scared she had been, as scared as he was, and while the moment was not even the end of this violent episode, it could be the beginning of something else. This was entirely different from the embrace in her kitchen, not half an hour ago. It was not about love or lust or even hope, but about survival.

A uniformed officer approached, and Alyssa let go of Reid and took a step back. Another emergency vehicle was in the garage now, a small square red truck unlike anything he'd seen in Chicago. "I'll have to go downtown," she said. "Let the paramedics check you out. If they want to take you to the hospital, go." Her tone was stern and commanding, what he imagined she used on the streets. She put out her hand and touched his cheek. "I'm glad you're not dead," she said, and then she left.

The officer asked him for a brief statement and steered him toward the paramedic van. His partner had bagged the knife, and they were stretching caution tape around the area, now a crime scene. Reid was surprised they hadn't asked for more information, but Alyssa would have told them the attack might be connected to Detective Macias's case. In the van he couldn't catch his breath and started to shake. There were two paramedics, a young man with a high forehead and military-cut dark hair and a plump, motherly woman about forty with a light brown ponytail. Their uniforms were similar to the CCPD's.

"Looks like shock," the young man said.

The woman had Reid lie down, checked for broken bones, took his pulse and blood pressure, and shone a penlight in his eyes. "No," she said. "It's only a stress reaction." She gave brisk instructions in a way that suggested the young man was a trainee, still learning under her tutelage. She spread the heated blanket he handed her over Reid and said, "You're okay. You're going to be okay," in a soothing, almost hypnotic voice. "Lie still for a minute until you get warm."

"I'm all right," he said. He felt spacey, groggy, as if this were all a dream and he was starting to wake up. He tried to sit up, and she put out a gentle hand to restrain him without force.

"You'll be fine," she agreed. She asked a few questions—"Did you hit your head? Did you lose consciousness?"—and looked into his eyes again before she let him sit up. She leaned in as if she didn't want the other paramedic to hear what she said. "Don't be afraid to cry," she said. "It's a great way to relieve traumatic stress. I know you macho types think it's not cool for guys, but it works."

She was right, of course. Men suffered more stress-related illnesses because women knew how to find relief in tears. He had read the book by Captain Phillips, who had struggled against tears every morning after he was kidnapped by Somali pirates until, on the advice of a psychiatrist, he had let go and got all the feelings out at once. But what Reid had been through was minor compared to such an ordeal. He had faced immediate danger for less than a minute, and the stress reaction was simply the aftermath of adrenaline. He might have been killed, but people were almost killed every day, often without even knowing it.

He didn't feel like crying, not then, and not after he got back to his apartment and sat for a while with his head in his hands, overwhelmed by the whole morning: Alyssa's ambivalence—"Don't say that. I love you too"—the sudden violence of the attack, and most of all the knowledge, not merely an idea now, but something he knew right down to his bones, that somebody had wanted to kill him.

What had happened in the garage was still a blur. Could Alyssa be strong enough, able to subdue a large, homicidal brute single-handed? Did she know karate? Had she somehow tripped the assailant? Had she had her gun? Was her police training enough without any of her equipment and dressed in a skirt and heels? What had she been doing while he was knocked out?

This might not be finished yet. He didn't know the reason for the attack, so how could he know whether someone else might still have the same intent? He rose and double-checked the deadbolt and chain, the window locks—he tried to open them, as Alyssa had advised—and the newly installed security bar on the balcony door. Would he ever feel safe again?

He took solace in his favorite distraction—cooking. He had a quarter ham and made a marmalade glaze, pineapple-mint relish, sweet potato biscuits, and a salad with radishes, green onions, and snap peas, an Easter feast worthy of his mother's kitchen and enough to feed three or four. He would be eating the leftovers all week. The ham and salad would make a good cold lunch, but the biscuits were best fresh out of the oven, slathered in sweet butter. He wished he could share the meal with Alyssa, but she would be at work by now, patrolling the mean streets. The heat of the kitchen was comforting, like being wrapped in a warm blanket, but while he sliced the ham, he remembered the glint of the knife in the dim garage and imagined his father and sister being notified of his death.

His appetite at least was not affected by what had happened. If anything, he ate more than usual—voracious emotional eating, the worst sin of the health-conscious dieter. He was enjoying a flaky buttered biscuit when his phone rang. He almost didn't answer—what if was a threat or a warning?—but when he looked at the caller ID the number was familiar.

"Reid, sweetie," Jane said, all sympathy and concern, and he closed his eyes, surprised by how deeply her kindness touched him. "Are you okay?"

He took a deep breath. "I'm fine. How are you?"

"I'm good. Do you need anything? Do you want company? Can I come over?"

He was surprised by his own reaction, by the warmth spreading through his chest. "Yes," he said. "I have a ton of food. Come help me eat it."

After he hung up, he regretted getting her out in the cooling evening air when she had so recently been ill, but he wasn't sorry she was coming. He put the biscuits back in the still-warm oven and set another place at the table. Why was it Jane and not Alyssa who called him? She had been dealing with the law enforcement end of things and had to work the evening shift, but she could have spared a minute to call him. Jane had called to ask him to take Alyssa what she needed when she was hurt—had Alyssa asked Jane to return the favor? He should consider her as Alyssa's representative and not assume she simply didn't care. Jane would report back to her.

When Jane rang the doorbell, he dutifully used the peephole, opened the door with the chain on, and made sure she was alone before he let her in. She was dressed modestly for a change, in jeans and a fuzzy sweater that was scratchily comforting when she put her arms around him. They stood together near the door without moving for a long time and parted with an unforced and unembarrassed laugh.

He took her into the kitchen and piled her plate high. "Oh, wait until I tell Liss about this," she cried.

"You can take her the leftovers," he said. "If there are any." In fact, his hunger was gone, and he sat back to enjoy watching her do justice to his efforts.

"Tell me everything," she said, as if it was a simple request, as if she just wanted some juicy gossip. It wasn't simple at all, but he told her everything he could. As he recited the tale, he remembered he hadn't told the police he might have recognized his assailant. They would surely have more questions for him later.

"Go on!" Jane cried. "The snappy dresser?"

"I could have imagined that part," he conceded. "It all seemed like a dream at the time."

"A nightmare, you mean."

She was a good listener, and he surprised himself by telling her more than the dramatic details of the scene in the parking garage, more than he had told Alyssa about Baird's murder, and even how things were between them now.

"Liss doesn't know her own mind," she said. "I'd give her more time, if I was you, but if you're ready to throw in the towel, I'm still available." She grinned cheekily.

"Thank you," he said. "That's good to know."

They talked for more than an hour, and it was the most satisfying conversation he had ever had with her and more comforting than she could have imagined. When they had eaten their fill and run out of immediate topics of conversation, she helped him box the leftovers for Alyssa, not even holding back a slice of ham for a sandwich. He thought she might leave then, but she put the box in the refrigerator, led the way to the living room, and claimed the remote. They watched three episodes of *Breaking Bad*, sitting side by side on the couch, with his hand in hers.

Finally, she turned off the TV and studied him gravely. "Want me to stay?" she asked.

"No," he said. "I'll be fine, Jane."

She took his face in her hands and kissed him on the mouth. "Are you sure?" she asked.

"I'm sure," he said, but he kissed her back. He had never kissed a woman with a nose piercing before, and he didn't much care if she was contagious.

She put a hand on his thigh. "Are you su-u-ure? Really, really sure?" He was, but he was also surprised by how tempted he was. "It's just sex," she coaxed. "It might make you feel better. It's like life-affirming or whatever."

"I'm sure you're right, but it's still no. I'm sorry."

"It's all right, sweetie," she said with an understanding smile. "If you don't want to, I could still stay. I can hold you or lie next to you, so you won't be alone tonight."

He could only think how much he would have loved such an offer from Alyssa. "I'm really okay."

"Well, then, do you want to get drunk?"

He had to laugh. "No, I don't. And you don't either, because you have to drive home, and trust me, you do not want a DUI. It's very inconvenient. All I have is cooking sherry anyway. Too much sodium."

"Okay, then," she said and slapped her knees, ready to rise.

"Thank you for coming. I mean it. I didn't even know it was what I needed, but it helped a lot. You're probably the best friend I have here."

Jane raised her eyebrows. "Probably?"

He conceded her point with a smile. "Definitely. You should go home and get some sleep now if you're going to work tomorrow. I'm sorry you had to come out when you weren't feeling well."

"Oh, I'm all better," she said blithely. She gave him a very sensuous kiss and sat back to study his face. "Still no?"

"Still no. Good night, Jane. Don't forget the leftovers."

Chapter Fifteen

Reid didn't sleep well, but he did sleep and considered it enough of an accomplishment. If he dreamed, the images fled as soon as he woke up—no berets, gas masks, or familiar blond strangers. He was still coming up against the blank wall of motive. If the killer was the man from the elevator, why would he want to kill him? Because he removed his hand from Jane's breast? Hardly a classic motive for murder. What was the connection with Baird? At least a financial motive might be involved in his death, not to mention Mrs. Baird's dalliance with Randy Goff, but there was no way on earth he could imagine Goff trying to kill anybody or hiring someone to do it for him, or any woman killing her husband to be with him.

He remembered Jane saying it would be funny if the guy in the elevator was his potential employer. What if, instead, he had been a fellow applicant? Could he be insane enough to want to kill the boss and the successful candidate for the job? Even in a struggling economy, it was a stretch. If the killer had instead been fired from the job Reid had taken, he might have motive to kill both the man who fired him and the usurper who took his place, but Reid was reasonably sure his job was the result of the business prospering and Baird wanting to expand.

What if the attack in the garage, whether or not it

was the man he thought he'd recognized, had nothing at all to do with the murder? Maybe they were two distinct cases with different motives and different perpetrators. Didn't criminals have habitual MOs? Wasn't a man who bashed one victim in the head unlikely to come after another with a car and a knife? But why would his picture be with what was believed to be the murder weapon, his name with Baird's license number?

Not until he was in the shower, hot water cascading over him, did the tears come. He told himself he was only releasing stress, but in a matter of seconds he was mourning all the losses in his life—his mother, Sarah, Chicago, Baird…and Alyssa, who was not lost, but was so far away when he wanted her closer and closer. The trouble with tears was once you started, there was always something else underneath wanting to come out. He cried because he had almost died and still didn't know who wanted to kill him, because he could still feel the fear and the adrenaline rush and the hardness of metal and concrete and the knowledge of some malevolent force that wanted to end his life, because he might be responsible in some way for Baird's death, and because he had been unable to take what Jane had so generously offered. He hadn't even cried over his mother's death before this. When he had had to call Emily in Texas and tell her, he had teared up a little, but nothing more.

Afterwards he felt better, if a little foolish. He considered calling in sick to prevent the awkwardness of not knowing what to say. Could he keep the secret from everyone at Conavard when some wider conspiracy might put them in danger too? And if he did tell anyone what happened, they would have a million questions, which he would have to answer with "I don't know." He decided to be practical. He had work to do, some of which could best be done at Conavard. Nobody was likely to ask probing questions. "How was your weekend?" was a question they wouldn't even want a reply to.

He was slicing plump, ripe strawberries for his granola when the doorbell rang. He took the usual precautions, even though Officer Alyssa Knight was visible through the peephole in her long-sleeved navy blue uniform and shiny badge, with her hair in a tight bun.

He took a deep breath and opened the door. "Good morning, Officer."

"Morning. How're you doing?"

"I'm good."

She held up the index and middle fingers of her right hand. "How many fingers?"

"Two." He gestured for her to follow him into the kitchen. On impulse, he picked up a strawberry and held it out, an inch from her lips. "Try one," he said. "They're very sweet."

She took a bite, almost brushing his fingers with her lips, and he watched intently while she ate it. "Oh, stop it," she said crossly. "Makes me feel like I'm in the zoo. Are you going to turn into one of those obsessive, creepy restraining-order cases?"

"I like that shade of lipstick," he said.

"Sure you do. You said you wouldn't stalk me."

The best defense was to ignore her words. "Want some breakfast?" he asked, indicating the table set for one.

"No, thanks," she said. "I'll grab something later.

Go ahead, please."

Reid took the milk out of the refrigerator. "You're working this morning after doing the evening shift last night? You couldn't have gotten much sleep."

"I don't do it very often." He poured the milk but wouldn't sit until she did. "I ate when I got home last night," she said. "Your ham and salad. It was very good."

"It was better hot."

"I like cold ham. So…somebody tries to kill you, and you go home and bake a ham?"

"It's what I do best."

"Okay, well…" She was ready to get down to business. "We don't know much yet, it being Easter and all. Bail hearing sometime today."

"They wouldn't let him out, would they?" He tried not to sound personally threatened.

She shrugged. "He's not talking yet, but Macias hasn't had a crack at him. His name is Tarik Facenda. Mean anything to you?"

He shook his head. He couldn't remember whether it was on the list Macias had shown him of Mrs. Baird's contacts, but it was distinctive enough to have stood out if it had been. "What kind of name is Tarik?"

"Arabic. He doesn't look Arabic, but people do all sorts of things to their kids. Look at you. Emerson Reid. Can't say I'm crazy about my name either."

"I like it."

"You would." It was her turn to watch him eat. "So did Jane console you last night?"

"Yes, as a matter of fact, she did. And no, we didn't."

"Knowing Jane, I'm sure she tried."

Reid took a bite of toast with almond butter to delay and to distract himself and couldn't help asking anyway, "What about me? Do you know me?"

Alyssa drummed her fingers on the table as she studied him. "Good question," was all she said in reply. "I'd better go. I'll let you know if I find out anything else."

"Will they want to talk to me again? The officers didn't ask me very much yesterday."

"Yeah, probably."

She was about to leave, and to hold her there a little longer, he said, "Alyssa? Would you like to go dancing Saturday night?"

"No," she said. "Friday's better."

"Friday, then."

"Where are we going? The Aurora? Just so I'll know what to wear."

"I thought the Aurora, unless you have a better idea. I liked the dress you wore last time. Pretty color."

"You liked taking it off," she said cynically. "We're not doing that again."

"Okay."

"Okay again. You're like a broken record. Don't you ever get angry?"

"Yes, of course I do."

"When?" she asked.

He tried to think of an example. He had been annoyed with Jane and with Randy Goff and with a customer who kept changing his mind. He had been sad, depressed, and resentful—but the white-hot anger he had seen flare up sometimes in others? He was sure he had but couldn't think of an example. Had he even been angry with Facenda? When Sarah was killed—

shock, guilt, devastation, but surely anger too, at the injustice, the unreasonable excess, the pointless, inexcusable jealousy, the violence against a woman who was totally innocent.

He had been silent too long. "I thought so," Alyssa said. "I get angry when I see children victimized, when somebody cuts me off on the freeway, when drunks wake me up to bail them out, even when I burn the toast."

"I don't burn the toast."

"Oh, I'm sure you don't. Paul used to make fun of me when I got all hot and bothered. He could be like ice when he was angry, but I'd always get flustered. I have to wonder what it's going to look like when all your repressed anger finally comes out."

"I'm not repressing anything, Alyssa."

"Yeah, you wear your heart on your sleeve," she said. "But…"

"But what? I'm pretty sure the theory about everybody needing to express anger or they'll get ulcers is outdated. You want me to get angry? You want me to yell and throw things? You want me to act like a caveman and throw you down on the bed when you say no? Is that what you like? If it is…"

"No, it isn't. I'm sorry. I'm just being cranky. I'd better go." She stood, gesturing for him to remain seated, and he couldn't help noticing the heavy belt she wore with its attached handcuffs and holster. This was not a woman to be trifled with.

She turned away, and his gaze slid from the belt to the way her pressed trousers fit. He was glad she couldn't see his face. She stopped in the doorway and looked back at him gravely, one hand on her hip. "It's called Ravishing Rose," she said.

"What?"

"My lipstick. It's called Ravishing Rose. Corny, huh?" She smiled and waved a hand. "See ya."

****

He didn't say anything at Conavard, but the secret was out when a police officer flashed her badge at the reception desk and asked for him. It wasn't Macias, but a sixtyish African-American woman who introduced herself as Detective Cartwright. She asked all the questions the officers at the scene hadn't covered, the ones even Alyssa hadn't asked. He told her he thought he'd recognized Facenda in the garage, but couldn't be sure, and she showed him a mug shot. It was him—the well-dressed man who had touched Jane. He had barely noticed his face when he got on the elevator, but the shape of his nose and the slant of his eyebrows were familiar.

"This is very important," Cartwright said approvingly. "Your testimony will place him in the building near the day of Baird's murder. And in the parking garage, you knew it was the same man?"

"Yes."

"Did he say anything to you?" she asked.

When he repeated the words Facenda had used, he remembered the moment all too vividly, and it was as if a dangerous shadow fell across the familiar office. The threat had been surreal at the time, but now the stark reality of it made him shudder. He was grateful that Detective Cartwright pretended not to notice.

Before she left, he asked her what would happen next with Facenda. "It's too soon to tell," she said, poker-faced. "He's on a no-bail hold because he violated parole, but the wheels of justice grind exceedingly slowly."

****

Alyssa loved the Aurora Ballroom. She loved the music the band played and being able to move to the rhythm, freely and easily. The lighting was soft, and the customers were usually well-behaved. She liked being with Reid, who was a decent dancer and held her very respectfully for someone who knew too much about her body. On the few occasions when she had been able to get Paul to take her dancing, he would be all hands and then unusually demanding when he got her alone.

She had told Reid she didn't miss sex, but it wasn't true. What she didn't miss was being punished in countless, subtle ways if she wasn't in the mood, forcing herself to participate when she felt badgered, and trying to express love she could no longer feel. She did miss the connection, another body close to hers, and she missed caring about someone enough to want his happiness.

Unlike Jane, she hadn't been with many men, but enough to know they weren't all like Paul. Reid, with all the cuddly warmth of a well-bred puppy, was the easiest. Not best, because making love was not about performance, as most men believed. It was about feelings. She didn't think sex meant the same thing to men as it did to women, and Reid behaved as if it did, as if he wanted what she wanted and could get it from her, of all women. Even the way he undressed her—had Paul ever taken the time, even in the early stages of their relationship, or had he always waited impatiently for her to disrobe? Most men wanted to satisfy women to prove their own virility. Reid seemed to want to give her pleasure, as he did when he cooked, and try as she might, she couldn't believe it was real.

Between dances, they sipped the innocuous, colorful drinks the bar had to offer, with bubbles that tickled her throat and rested uneasily in her stomach, and they made conversation, more naturally than the first time, when the artificial construct of a "date" had made her want to kick against the traces and give him a hard time. He was trying to get to know her in a first date kind of way, as if he needed to ground her in reality and haul his fantasy back to earth. She was all for that and answered his mundane questions with amused patience. He wanted to know what kind of movies she liked, what she read, where she had traveled.

"When is your birthday?"

"Oh, like what's my sign?"

He shook his head. "I want to make you a fabulous birthday dinner."

"July eighteenth."

"Summer barbecue season," he said. "Sweet-and-spicy baby back ribs, baked beans in a tomato-and-brown-sugar sauce, fresh corn on the cob, lemon-garlic potato salad, sliced tomatoes, sweet pickles, homemade bread, a double chocolate layer cake…"

"You had me at chocolate."

"How many candles?" he asked.

"Twenty-six," she said. "The whole menu sounds delicious, but I know you have an ulterior motive."

"You're too young to be so cynical," he said. "Somebody made you this way."

"Don't psychoanalyze me," she said. "I like it better when you talk about cooking. Let's dance." The band had struck up a mambo, a dance they both enjoyed, and for the next few minutes everything was natural and easy between them, their movements free and perfectly synchronized. He smiled as he swung her around, and she liked the way her soft jersey skirt flowed with her. She felt pretty and feminine and carefree and wanted the feeling to last forever.

The next one was slower, and she let her hand drift to the back of his neck, felt the clean, thick texture of his hair under her fingers, and rested her head on his shoulder as they turned and swayed to the music of a smooth, romantic guitar solo. It was all too good to be true, but it would be nice while it lasted.

They didn't stay out late because she had to work the next day, and as they headed back to the parking lot, Reid said, "If you'll come up for coffee, I have some macadamia nut brownies to go with it."

"Oh, so you can show me your etchings?" she asked. She loved macadamia nuts and was always a sucker for brownies, but she was sure it wasn't a good idea. She was nervous, not because she was afraid of Reid, who was as harmless a man as she could imagine, but because she didn't trust herself.

"Just coffee," he said. "I don't want the evening to end yet."

"If it's coffee you want," she said, "we can have it at my place. I don't have any brownies, but there are some chocolate chip cookies. I'll drive you home after, but I won't go upstairs with you."

"Don't you trust me?" he asked.

"Yes, as a matter of fact I do. I'm still not going upstairs, but I'll watch to make sure nobody else ambushes you in the garage."

****

Reid sat on the couch, feeling stiffly formal in the rarely used living room, and waited until Alyssa came out of the kitchen with the silver tray. Two large white china mugs steamed invitingly next to a plate of cookies—store-bought, he could tell. "This is just coffee," she said. "Jane and I have a rule about bringing men back here."

"I've been here lots of times."

"You know what I mean."

"Okay. I don't want you to break any rules." He sipped his coffee. It was fine, but he could make better. They chatted for a while, about dancing and about work, and he tried one of the cookies and pretended he liked it.

Alyssa gave him a smile that suggested she wasn't fooled. She was knowing and affectionate and so pretty he couldn't resist her. He put a hand on her knee and leaned in to kiss her. Her mouth was soft and willing, and he put down the coffee cup and took her face in both hands.

After a long, intense interval of suspended time, she pulled away and rested her forehead against his. "Oh, Reid," she said—half disapproval, half sighing acquiescence. He stroked her breast, and her breathing quickened, and he slid a hand over her nylon-clad knee and under her skirt to find bare thigh. "Don't," she said.

He paused but didn't withdraw his hand. "Is that no?" he asked.

She sighed. "Not yet," she said, but she was warning him too, not to go too far, beyond the point of no return. Only it was hard to know where that was. She didn't touch him, but after a minute more of intense kissing, her hand slid over his and guided it where she wanted him to touch. It was time, past time, to relocate to the bedroom, but he still expected her to stop him. A minute later she did—she said, "Shit!" and straightened up, away from him.

"Tell me what you want me to do," he said.

"I don't know!" She rose quickly, walked a few steps away, and then turned back to take his hand again.

They adjourned to the bedroom, the pretty room with blue curtains, where he had fed her bean soup and gnocchi not so long ago. She still had a small white scar on the bridge of her nose, easily covered by makeup when she made the effort. He touched it, remembering, and she didn't flinch because she had learned to trust him, and then she was undressing him, and the white comforter was thrown aside, and the cool, blue-striped sheets lay invitingly exposed.

She was right with him all the way, and it was so sweet, so easy, like a dance to unheard music. He wanted her, and he wanted even more to please her, not to disappoint her in any way, to do everything she liked and nothing she didn't, to explore every inch of her lovely skin, to learn her body and all its secrets and love her the way she deserved to be loved. What she gave in return was both irrelevant and priceless.

Afterward, she sat up and put her head in her hands. "Why do I keep doing this?" she asked fretfully.

"Because you like it?" he suggested. He watched her attentively, hopefully.

"No, I don't. It just makes things worse. Get dressed. I'll take you home." He didn't budge. He wanted to stay. "You can't be here when Jane gets home," she said sharply.

"Okay, but don't get up," he said. "I'll take the bus." He slid to the edge of the bed to pull on his pants.

"It's dangerous to take the bus this time of night."

"Not with Facenda locked up."

"What if you get mugged for your cell phone or your wristwatch?"

"I'll take a taxi, then." He bent and kissed her. "I'm sorry if you regret this, but I don't. I love you."

"Oh, shut up," she said crossly. She started to get out of bed, but she changed her mind and stayed where she was. As he left the room, she said, "Be careful. Please."

Chapter Sixteen

Alyssa showed up at Reid's door again on Tuesday morning, and this time she let him make her a modest breakfast: oatmeal with blueberries, brown sugar, and pecans, an English muffin with peanut butter, and mochaccino because she loved chocolate. She was off today, and she wore jeans and a plain pink T-shirt, her beautiful hair brushed and shining and unrestrained.

She had a large manila envelope, which she didn't explain. While they ate, she told him Facenda had copped to attempted murder, but denied any knowledge of Baird's death. "He was promised a plea deal, and Macias tried to convince him the evidence against him is sufficient for a murder conviction. It isn't—his fingerprints don't match any found at the scene—but Macias is a pretty good bluffer."

"I wouldn't say that. He tried with me, and I wasn't convinced. If the fingerprints don't match, does it mean he didn't do it?"

"It could mean lots of things. Probably he did it, but maybe somebody else was involved."

"So, what would a plea deal mean?"

"With first degree, usually taking the death penalty off the table, or it might be the possibility of parole, but it's not always about the sentence. I don't know all the details, but I think they promised him something for pleading guilty to the lesser charge too. You'd be surprised what suspects will ask for. To tell their families the bad news in person, to serve the sentence at a particular prison, all kinds of things. One guy confessed to burglary for a sausage pizza. I know I'd confess for chocolate layer cake."

"Duly noted."

She took a bite of her English muffin, thickly spread with rich peanut butter. "I don't understand," she said. "Why aren't you fat? You could stand to lose a *few* pounds, but when you eat like this all the time and have a sedentary job? I'd be all roly-poly."

"I'd like to see you roly-poly."

"No, you wouldn't. You wouldn't lust after me then."

"Yes, I would."

She ignored him. "Seriously, why aren't you fat?"

"Metabolism, I guess. My mom was always thin."

"And your dad?"

"Isn't my biological father."

"Oh! Oh, I'm sorry."

"Don't be. He's my dad in every other way." Reid refilled her coffee cup and offered her another muffin, but she shook her head.

"I don't know why I'm surprised," she said. "I guess I assumed you came from a long line of Emersons and Reids and whatnot."

"Actually, I was named after the poet—my mother was an English major—and John Reid, better known as the Lone Ranger."

Alyssa laughed, delighted. The color of her eyes deepened, and the lines of her face were all soft and curved. He couldn't help smiling back. "The Lone Ranger? I knew I would like your mother," she said.

"What does your stodgy dad think of that?"

"I'm not sure he got the joke."

"What's your sister's name?"

"Emily Dickinson Lucas."

"Oh, of course. At least I get *her*. Emerson is beyond me."

"I'm not fond of him myself," he said, which made her smile again.

When they were finished eating, she took a stapled sheaf of papers out of the manila envelope. "I didn't give you this," she said.

Tape Recorded Interview

Tarik Matthew Facenda /Detective Dale Macias

DM *This is Detective Macias, Carroll City Police Department. Today's date is Thursday, May 2ⁿᵈ. The time is 9:51 A.M. This will be a taped conversation with last name of Facenda, F-A-C-E-N-D-A, first of Tarik, T-A-R-I-K, middle of Matthew, M-A-T-T-H-E-W. Date of birth 12-08-83. Mr. Facenda, I am taping this conversation so I don't have to take notes. I have advised you of your rights, and you have signed a waiver form. Is that correct?*

TF *Yes.*

DM *We'll be going over some of what you've already told us, but this is for the official record, and you'll have a chance to review the statement before you sign it. Are you okay with this being taped?*

TF *Yeah, whatever.*

DM *Okay, I'm gonna start with some easy questions. Do you recognize the name Reid Lucas?*

TF *Yes.*

DM *You know who I'm referring to? Mr. Emerson Reid Lucas, native of Chicago, now residing in Carroll*

City?

TF *Yeah, yeah. I'm not stupid.*

DM *I'm very glad to hear that. When did you first become aware of this individual by name?*

TF *[indistinct]*

DM *Could you speak up, please? I didn't quite hear.*

TF *This guy I met in prison.*

DM *What guy is that?*

TF *This guy Oldham. Freddy Oldham.*

DM *What did he tell you about Mr. Lucas?*

TF *He was doin' his old lady, so Freddy offed her.*

Reid looked up at Alyssa, appalled. "Oh, my God," he said, and remembering too late, "I'm sorry."

"I'll assume it was a prayer," she said. "I know this is awful, but God will forgive you." It was a strange thing to say when he was the victim here, but she knew that the motive and everything that had led to Baird's murder was his doing. He understood now where the picture found with the tire iron had come from—cut out of a group shot at a party where he had stood next to Sarah.

"Will *you?*" he asked.

"I wouldn't have if you'd let him kill you. Didn't I tell you it was dangerous to mess with married women?"

DM *Mr. Oldham told you Mr. Lucas was having sexual relations with Mrs. Oldham?*

TF *Yeah.*

DM *And on learning about this, he murdered her?*

TF *Yeah. Broke her neck.*

DM *How did you feel about that?*

TF *Wasn't my business.*

DM *So you didn't feel personally offended by her behavior?*

TF *No, but I got why he was.*

DM *What else did Mr. Oldham say to you about Mr. Lucas?*

TF *That when I got out, I should finish the job. As a favor because he was decent to me. Had my back. We were both from Chicago, y'know. People tend to hang with their own kind.*

DM *He wanted you to finish the job? What did you understand that to mean?*

TF *Off him.*

DM *Meaning Mr. Lucas?*

TF *Yes.*

DM *And did you agree to do it? Is that a nod to indicate yes?*

TF *Yes.*

DM *Did he indicate how you should go about "offing" Mr. Lucas?*

TF *Just not to get caught, to make it look like an accident or like a robbery or whatever, not to cast suspicions on myself or him.*

DM *Meaning Mr. Oldham?*

TF *Yes.*

DM *And did you subsequently get out of prison?*

TF *I'm here, ain't I?*

DM *So it seems. Did you then decide to carry out this favor for Mr. Oldham?*

TF *Yeah.*

DM *How did you set about doing this?*

TF *Oldham knew some people who knew Lucas, and I asked around about him like he was a friend of mine. Somebody told me he got laid off his job and was* *going to interview for one in California. So, I like pretended I knew about computers and shit, and if this company was hiring, they might have more than one job open, and got the name. Figured it would be perfect— do the job in California, no connection to me or Freddy. Lucas goes to California and gets offed, bad luck for him, nothin' to do with us.*

DM *But you were on parole and not supposed to leave Illinois, isn't that right?*

TF *Yeah, so the cops wouldn't think I coulda been here.*

DM *How did you get here?*

TF *Southwest Airlines.*

DM *But these days you need ID to fly.*

TF *Yeah, Homeland Security and shit. I used my cousin's ID. He looks a lot like me, and I knew they wouldn't look too close. Nobody's driver's license picture looks that much like them. Told you I ain't stupid.*

DM *Yes, you're very clever. So, you flew to Carroll City the day of the interview?*

TF *Two days before. Called the computer place to confirm the time of the appointment and scoped out the building.*

DM *That would be the building at 1049 Jefferson St., where the Conavard Software offices are located?*

TF *Yeah, something like that. I waited in the lobby, sat and pretended to read the paper, but I kept an eye on the door.*

DM *This was on the afternoon of January 21ˢᵗ?*

TF *Yeah. Martin Luther King Day.*

DM *And you had the murder weapon with you? The tire iron?*

TF I told you I don't know about any tire iron. I had a knife. I had it in a briefcase or like a computer case. I was in disguise as a hotshot businessman.

DM You worked at a car wash. How did you pay for the airline ticket and the fancy duds?

TF Oldham give me some money. He was like rich and connected in Chicago.

DM You mean like mob connected?

TF No, like legit business, but serious money. He had somebody bankroll me, pay for the airline ticket and motel, and he was gonna give me a lot of cash when the job was done. I didn't do it for the money, though. It was a favor. I didn't pay for the clothes. Only chumps pay for shit like that.

DM You mean you stole the clothes?

TF Yeah, y'know, used some sucker's credit card. So anyway, Lucas comes in, and I follow him onto the elevator.

DM How did you know it was him?

TF I knew what he looked like. Freddy Oldham showed me a picture.

DM Did he give you the picture? Did you have it with you?

TF No, but I got a good memory for faces. So anyway, I get on the elevator with him, and I was gonna do it right there, but this woman got on too. Didn't want a witness.

Reid looked up from the page. "Jane saved my life," he said.

"And then I had to do it again," Alyssa pointed out. "This time you'd better stay saved."

DM So what did you do?

TF I got off the elevator and went downstairs and

177

waited for Lucas to come out, but he never did. Musta left another way or something, so I split.

DM *You gave up?*

TF *I didn't give up. I was being cautious. Decided it would be better to find another place to do it anyway, in case the building had security cameras. I hadda go back to Chicago first to meet with my parole officer, go to work, stuff like that.*

DM *You went directly back to Chicago?*

TF *Yeah, the next day.*

DM *So there will be a record of you—or your cousin—taking a flight the following day?*

TF *I don't know what kind of records airlines keep. There's a stewardess who would remember me, though.*

DM *Yeah, right. But according to you, you were no longer in Carroll City on Saturday, January 26th, when Victor Baird was killed?*

TF *I don't know about any Victor Baird. I told you I had nothing to do with him.*

DM *You wouldn't hold out on me, would you, Tarik?*

TF *If I'm lyin', I'm dyin'.*

DM *Uh-huh. So, what did you do then?*

TF *When I got ready to try again, I called this computer place and asked for Lucas to make sure he worked there, and then I flew back to California.*

DM *On or around April 21st?*

TF *Yeah, Easter week. The boss's kid was on spring break, and he had him working my shifts.*

DM *How did you set about carrying out your intentions?*

TF *I found out where the dude lived, rented a car,*

and went to his building and waited for him. Everybody was doing Easter stuff, family shit and church and like that, or sleeping late. It was real quiet in the garage.

"Where's the rest?" Reid asked. He wanted Facenda's account of the attack, if only to see Alyssa through the eyes of the man she had bested.

"You know the rest," she said. "You don't need to read it, and you didn't read this either. You never saw it. I never saw it." She took the sheaf of pages from him and slid them back in the envelope.

She stood up to leave, and he automatically rose too. She put up a hand to suggest he didn't need to follow her to the door and then, as if she'd had a change of heart, leaned in to give him a kiss on the lips.

It was quick and unemotional, but her soft hair brushed his cheek, and he could detect vanilla-scented soap or body lotion on her skin and taste her lipstick. Ravishing Rose, he remembered.

He was late to work, but it was worth it.

Chapter Seventeen

On Wednesday, Randy Goff stood leaning against his car two spaces down from where Reid parked. He gave him a patently insincere smile. "Good morning."

"Morning," Reid echoed. "What's up?"

They started to walk together toward the elevator. "A meeting is scheduled at nine, but I wanted to give you a heads-up, so you won't be blindsided."

"Okay." Did Goff think they were pals now? He knew better. Goff always had an agenda.

"The good news is Gloria has decided to keep Conavard going. It's what Baird would want. And…" He paused for effect and added with a sly look, "She's putting me in charge."

Reid was too surprised to be tactful. "Why? We all thought Heyerdahl…Oh."

Goff grinned. "Yeah."

"Uh…congratulations."

"And then there's the bad news."

"Which is?" But he had a sinking feeling in the pit of his stomach.

"I'm afraid we have to let you go."

Reid took the blow in silence. Their footsteps were loud in the echoing space of the garage. "Why?" he asked finally.

"Budget concerns, of course," Goff said smoothly. "Y'know, last hired, first fired." It didn't ring entirely true—Conavard was doing better than ever. "And of course," he added, "you brought your dirty Chicago business here."

"All I did was what you're doing," he pointed out, although in point of fact, he hadn't even done that.

"I guess you picked the wrong woman," Goff said with a smirk. "Better luck next time. I know it's not your fault Baird was killed, but you can imagine how Gloria feels."

"Is she unhappy with my work?"

"She doesn't have a clue about the work. Don't worry—we'll give you a great reference and a severance bonus, of course. It's nothing personal, Lucas. I'm only carrying out her wishes."

****

After the meeting, Reid cleared out his desk, called clients to tell them who would take over for him, and delivered his files to Goff. He did his best to keep a stiff upper lip, to pretend the job meant nothing to him beyond a paycheck. He drove out to the job site where he had expected to spend much of the day, to say goodbye and explain in person what would happen with the project.

His Conavard obligations taken care of, he drove home, but he couldn't stay in the apartment for more than a few minutes. He took the bus to Jane and Alyssa's apartment, knowing it was foolish not to at least call first. Jane would be at work, and Alyssa had the day off, but he had no reason to suppose she would be sitting at home. She might be out shopping, visiting her mother, almost anything.

She *was* home. Her Sonic was parked in front, and she answered the doorbell in jeans and a green Carroll

City Zoo T-shirt with a penguin on it. She was a little confused, but invited him in. "Why are you here?" she asked. "Shouldn't you be at work?"

"I'm out of a job," he said.

"What do you mean? Why?" She gestured for him to follow her into the kitchen.

"Have you seen the movie, *Nine to Five*? Lily Tomlin—'I killed the boss. You think they're not going to fire me for a thing like that?' "

"You didn't kill Baird. You were a victim." She had been doing laundry in the alcove off the kitchen, and she fetched an armload of T-shirts, fragrant from the dryer sheet, to the table to fold while they talked.

Reid sat across from her. "A not-so-innocent victim," he said. "I should have apologized to Mrs. Baird, but I didn't know what I could say without making things worse."

"I'm sorry," she said, her eyes soft with sympathy. "That sucks. What are you going to do?"

"Go back to Chicago, I guess." He waited to see if the idea would dismay her, but her expression didn't change.

"You don't have a job there either," she said.

"No, but I have family and friends, business contacts…"

"Which didn't help you get a job before."

"It won't hurt either. I miss Chicago. I even miss the weather."

"I'm sorry," she said. "I thought you liked it here."

"I don't suppose…you would go with me? My dad would love you, and opportunities for women in the police department have never been better. They would be lucky to have you, and you wouldn't be in your father's shadow the way you are here. Here you'll always be Captain Sharpe's daughter."

"Reid," she said, as to a naughty child who should know better. "I never led you on, did I? I told you from the beginning I didn't want a relationship, any kind of relationship. I think I was very clear on that subject. I certainly don't want to *live* with you. Even if I did, I wouldn't go to Chicago. My life is here. I was born here. My mother is here."

"She doesn't even know who you are."

She bit her lip. "It doesn't matter. She might…sometimes. And she still needs me. Anyway, it's irrelevant, because I told you—"

"I love you, Alyssa."

"No, you don't. You can't. You don't even know me. You love some silly, idealized idea of me you cooked up like a chocolate soufflé because you were lonely in a strange town. Now you can go home, and you won't need the fantasy anymore. Or you can stay here. There are jobs here too. And you do have friends here. Your neighbors like you, and some of your co-workers should still be friendly."

"I killed the boss."

"Stop saying that. They won't see it that way. Anyway, you can take me dancing and cook for Jane and get a better job than Conavard."

"I want more," he said.

"It's not going to happen. I hate to sound like a total cliché, but it's not you—it's me. I don't want to go through the whole compatibility test thing again."

"Test?"

"Oh, you know. How do our schedules mesh? Who cleans the refrigerator? What things do we both like?

183

What will we fight about? Are you going to belittle my faith? Will I resent you for not sharing it? What will make the other one crazy? All those little quirks you think are cute at first can drive you nuts in the long run. I already did it with Paul and then Jane. It's exhausting. At least with Jane I have my own bedroom."

"We'll have two incomes," he said, trying to be practical. "We could afford a two-bedroom place, if that's what you want."

"What do *you* want?" Alyssa asked. "Just for once can't you stick up for yourself? What do you want?"

"I want to love you."

"Worship at my feet? That could get old."

"I want to cook for you," he said. "I want to know you."

She appeared to like the sentiment, but she still had a stubborn expression. "You want to have sex," she said.

"Yes. I'm not going to pretend I don't want to make love with you. I want to hold you all night and wake up next to you in the morning. I want to go out dancing and to the zoo and Quique's and watch TV in bed and eat popcorn on a rainy day and play Scrabble and have a picnic on the beach and touch the place above your upper lip and—"

"Man, you're good. How did Sarah ever resist you?"

"Don't talk about Sarah," he warned.

"You *can* speak up for yourself," she said.

"Sarah is dead. It was over before it started. I want to talk about now."

"She still matters to you."

"Yes," he said. He got up, too agitated to sit still.

"Two people died. Will anyone die because I love you?"

"I've never seen you like this," she said.

"I've never *been* like this," he said. "I'm sorry I bothered you. I'll let myself out."

"Reid," she said, following him into the living room. "You're angry."

He turned and looked at her. She was frowning and biting her lip, upset or at least annoyed with him, and she was as pretty as ever. "Yes, I suppose I am."

"Now we know what you do when you're angry," she said bitterly. "You leave."

He should have stayed to show her she was wrong, but he wasn't sure she was. He left. He *was* angry. He was angry with Alyssa and with Goff and Mrs. Baird and most of all with himself for once again bashing his head against the stone wall of an unattainable woman. This one wasn't married, not as more than a technicality, but she wanted to be friends, and he wanted so much more.

He wished he was back in Chicago this very minute, but he still had two months left on his lease, and unless he wanted to drive across the country, he would need to sell his car. The Conavard severance pay would give him time to deal with things and find another job.

Carroll City was not home in any sense of the word. The weather was nice, in a bland, monotonous way, and he liked the Crown Ridge neighborhood well enough. The bus system was good, but he wouldn't need to depend on public transit much longer. This town was above all a place of failure. He had failed to keep a job, failed to develop a relationship, failed to find his place in the community. He had besmirched his otherwise clean driving record. Someone had tried to kill him here, and someone had died in his place.

He roamed the streets of his adopted city—no, not adopted. He had not made that much of a commitment. A foster city at best. Crown Ridge at least was familiar now, and he could find his way to a number of other places by bus, but it would never be home the way Chicago was.

He was sure Alyssa felt the same way about Carroll City. He could take the girl out of California, but she would still be a California girl. She would hate Chicago's winters, the bracing cold, the northeasterly winds, the falling snow, the very things he missed. He shouldn't have suggested she go with him, and he was sure he wouldn't have made such a mistake if he hadn't been in a state. He would have to apologize. If she wasn't unwilling to be friends after this, he would still be able to cook a birthday dinner for her before his lease was up.

Then he would go back to Chicago, reconnect with people—his father, Noah, other friends and co-workers—see the shrink Noah had recommended to deal with his survivor's guilt, ride the L, feel the wind off the lake, go to the Brookfield zoo, and think of Alyssa here in the sunshine.

He stood at a bus stop and watched a man in a red shirt walking a small black dog, and two young boys, one white, one black, showing off on their skateboards, and reflected on this temperate, still alien city. The weather was nice, but boring, the history rich but much different than in the Midwest. He had noticed fewer African Americans here, and of course more Latinos. If he stayed in Carroll City, he should learn Spanish. He could easily get a head start by reading all the bilingual signs. Going back to Chicago would make more sense. Nothing was holding him here.

He boarded one bus and then another and without reasoning anything out, he found himself back in a place not yet completely familiar, but with very strong associations for him—St. Anthony's Catholic Church. The nave was much quieter than on the two Sundays he had attended with Alyssa. This must be why she liked to come here after a stressful day on the streets, still in her uniform. He sat in a pew near the altar, took in the peaceful, welcoming beauty of the place, and mused on why he was here at all. Why had he come so far from home to take this job? What was he running from?

With or without the DUI, his whole time in Carroll City was a kind of probation, and he had served his sentence. It was time to go home. The ghost of Sarah was still there, but Baird's was here. Oldham had proved to be the psycho Alyssa had labeled him, and it might be true that he would have killed his wife eventually anyway. It was all very well to believe that, but what *he* had done had provided the immediate motive, and even if it hadn't, it was still very wrong. As he sat in the reverent quiet of the church, his transgression was as clear to him as it had always been to the church, to civilized society as a whole.

Thou shalt not commit adultery. To poach another man's wife, however dissatisfied she might be, to tempt her to break solemn vows just because he had taken a fancy to her. How would he feel if he was married to a woman like Alyssa, and another man…? The possibility was enough to make him break out in a cold sweat. He had wronged Sarah, not by causing her death, but by assuming he had a right to approach her in the first place. She had forgiven him. Oldham had not, but he was not the injured party. A woman was not a piece of property, whatever men like Oldham—and Paul Knight—might think. It was Sarah he had sinned against.

He didn't know if his thoughts would have taken the same direction if he hadn't come to St. Anthony's, but he was glad he had. Everything was simpler here, clearer. He offered a heartfelt prayer for forgiveness without any expectation of anyone hearing him. Did it matter whether you called it prayer or meditation?

Chapter Eighteen

Alyssa sat with her mother's hand in hers, but she was thinking about Reid. She had a very uneasy feeling, not her police-trained instinct for trouble, but something similar. He had said he wouldn't stalk her, but something dangerously obsessive underlay the way he had spoken to her this morning, his ridiculous declaration of love followed by a cold, hard anger.

Maybe he was just upset about losing his job—being fired could shake a person to the core, especially when he had come halfway across the country to take the position. Maybe he had made a grab for the only anchor he could find here. She couldn't blame him if he was confused about her feelings for him. She had given nothing but mixed signals ever since she had served Paul with the divorce papers.

Reid didn't seem like the kind of man who would become a stalker—very far from it—but who would have expected him to be almost killed on behalf of a jealous husband? Love was a dangerous game and could shatter more lives than wars and pandemics. She saw the victims every day—women who had risked everything and now stood behind ineffective restraining orders, children who cowered and wept while their parents threatened to tear each other apart.

"Meg?" her mother said plaintively, tugging at her hand.

"No, Mom, it's Alyssa," she said patiently.

"That's my daughter's name."

"Yes, you're right." She stood and leaned down to kiss the dry, papery skin of her mother's forehead. "Did you want Meg? She's in the other room. I can get her for you if you want."

"She takes care of me."

"Yes, she does. I can take care of you too if you'll let me. Can I get you something?"

Her mother gazed at her with a puzzled, almost suspicious expression. "Who are you?" she asked.

Alyssa took a deep breath. "I'm Alyssa, Mom. Your daughter."

"Oh. Alyssa. You never come to see me," she said fretfully.

"I come to see you all the time." She tried not to sound defensive, but her eyes filled with tears. "I'm here now."

"You look so pretty," her mother said, smiling. "What a pretty girl you are. Wait till Daddy sees how pretty you are in that dress."

She bit her lip to keep from pointing out that her pretty dress was a penguin T-shirt. Maybe her mother remembered a different day, a younger Alyssa, a special dress for a special day. She held a few of those in her own memories. One stood out—a sky-blue dress with a knee-length skirt in which she had felt passably pretty and very happy. Her father had taken one look and told her to take it off. He wouldn't have any daughter of his going out in public dressed like a cheap tart. She still felt both daring and a bit guilty when she wore a pretty dress. Ironically, she now saw the Catholic school uniform her father approved parodied all the time by streetwalkers.

"I'll get Meg for you," she said, gave her mother's cold hand a last squeeze, and went to the door.

"Tell my daughter to come see me," the frail woman instructed. "She never comes. I miss her."

"So do I," Alyssa said and left in search of the home health aide.

She went from her parents' house to church, as she often did, not so much to pray as to take a few minutes to settle her emotions. It was so hard to watch her mother waste away physically and mentally, not in a straight-line progression, but with ups and downs that kept her uncertain of what she would find each time.

When she visited St. Anthony's this early, she often had the nave to herself. Today she didn't. Two people were already inside. At the very back, a gray-haired woman in a thin lavender jacket knelt with a rosary in her hands, and a man was sitting in the second row. She glanced at him and away and then back again, caught by a sense of unexpected familiarity, but it took several seconds for her to recognize the hair covering the collar of the shirt she had seen him in this morning. She blinked, disbelieving, and he was still there. She stood where she was, paralyzed by uncertainty, until she was sure she didn't want him to know she was there. Why was he here? She couldn't understand. The woman with the rosary looked up, and Alyssa gave her a polite nod. She stood for another minute in the aisle, watching Reid, before she slipped out again.

It was not the healing she had come in search of, but it mattered. It mattered to her in a real and very profound way.

****

As he left St. Anthony's Reid remembered that

Jane considered Alyssa crazy to come here—what kind of background had she come from to make her feel that way? Jane didn't talk much about her past. She preferred to live in the present. Maybe he should learn to do the same.

He would be stupid not to want Jane in his life. Maybe he should call her and let her comfort him tonight. She appreciated his cooking more than Alyssa did anyway. He should have asked her to go to Chicago with him. She would enjoy the adventure. *Girls just want to have fun.* She could get a better job in Chicago, and he could cook for her every day, and she could warm his bed every night. It would do them both good. She wouldn't be faithful, which was what he deserved, and she would move on soon enough, but she might tide him over a few difficult months. Of course, his father would think he had taken leave of his senses...

Alyssa would have to find another roommate if she couldn't make a go of it on her own. She would miss Jane, and maybe she would miss him—and could he have a more selfish, childish train of thought? Asking Jane to go to Chicago was a very attractive idea—and he wasn't going to do it.

He drove home and started the daunting task of finding a job. He put out e-mail feelers in Chicago, searched for opportunities online, and to hedge his bets perused the classified ads in the *Carroll City Clarion*. Then he made a shopping list and headed to the nearby grocery store, with a brief stop at the library. He would spend the evening reading, lose himself in another world, and order pizza to eat with a small salad, but first he would make a chicken enchilada casserole for the Halvorsens on the fourth floor. Ramona was weeks from delivering her baby, and cooking dinner every night had become an arduous chore for her.

He sautéed diced sweet onion and poblano peppers in hot oil, enjoying the mellow, spicy odors and feeling the relief of tension cooking could always bring him. He had just added minced garlic when Jane called. "Reid, sweetie!" she cried. "You got fired?"

"Let go," he said. "Budget considerations."

"Like we don't know the real reason." Apparently, she could hear the sizzle of oil and said, "You're cooking?"

"Yes," he said, tucked the phone between his shoulder and neck to free both hands, and reached for a can of cream of chicken soup.

"What ya cooking?" she asked, and before he could answer, "Who's going to help you eat it?" She sounded very hopeful.

"It's for the neighbors." He struggled to work the can opener without dropping the phone. He wished he had a hands-free gadget like Jane and Alyssa's.

"Oh. What are you doing?" She must have noticed his difficulty.

"Opening a can."

"Oh. Are you okay? Want company tonight?"

"No, thank you. I have things to do." *Read. Feel sorry for myself.*

"You're gonna go back to Chicago?" she asked.

"That's the plan. Wanna come with me?" It was a reckless impulse, logical in the moment.

"Oh, sweetie!" she said with such warmth and sympathy he couldn't say a word in response. He noisily opened another can of soup. "We both know I'm not the one you want."

"It would be fun," he managed to say, but the argument sounded weak even to him.

"Liss doesn't like to be pushed or guilted into things," she said. She was right, of course. Alyssa was divorcing a passive-aggressive guy, and her father had nothing to say to her in church on Easter Sunday except to chide her for a missed visit with her mother.

"You're smarter than you look," he told Jane. She giggled. He almost dropped the phone and opened a can of diced green chilies.

"I can tell you're busy," she said. "I'll let you go, but do not run off to Chicago without saying goodbye."

"No, of course I won't."

"Promise?"

"I promise."

"Okay, sweetie. Good night. Feel better." She hung up, and he sighed and dropped the phone. Jane was a bracing gust of fresh air. It was too damned bad he couldn't fall in love with her.

An hour later, he carried the steaming casserole downstairs to the Halvorsens' apartment. Ramona, enormous in a shapeless pink dress, all but cried with gratitude. She stood awkwardly with both hands against the small of her back while he set the dish on a hot pad. "It needs to cool for about fifteen minutes," he said. "If you're not ready to eat by then, reheat it for five minutes or so when you are."

"This is so nice of you," Ramona said.

"It was entirely my pleasure," he assured her. He was about to leave when Tom walked into the kitchen. They exchanged perfunctory greetings, and Tom put a possessive arm around Ramona. He couldn't have known Reid had a penchant for married women, but he had an air of distrust for a man who would cook his wife dinner, even when she was about to burst with what looked like twins. Seeing himself through the husband's eyes shamed him. He remembered how much Tom loved sports and asked, "Dodgers playing San Francisco tonight?"

Tom relaxed a bit and launched into a monologue about the prospects for a win. As soon as he wound down, Reid made his exit. He returned to his apartment and ordered pizza and tried to get into the new Gillian Flynn novel, but all he could think about was Alyssa. He distracted himself with thoughts of cooking…what he would like to cook for her.

Chapter Nineteen

At the end of May, Reid navigated the last few hoops at the DMV and applied for a permanent California driver's license. Ironically, even though the offense had been committed in California, his Illinois license had been suspended for a whole year. If he moved back to Chicago, he couldn't get a new Illinois license for several months yet. Chicago had good public transit, so not being able to drive was not what was keeping him here until his lease was up.

Being able to drive anywhere he wanted was freeing, but he had to deal with the ignition interlock device every time. It would be a drag when he started dating again. One of the first places he planned to drive was the apartment on Ocean View. The Halvorsens had given him the idea—to take Alyssa and Jane a casserole as a thank you for their kindness to a stranger in a strange land.

He kept his pure motive in mind as he added macaroni to boiling water, chopped green pepper, and shredded cheddar cheese, but while he browned the ground beef he contemplated Alyssa trying this dish, putting a fork between her sweet lips, a cautious expression on her face, reserving judgment until she had tasted his latest offering. He hoped she would like this one. She would be too polite to say so if she didn't, but if she did, she would smile as only she could smile, and her eyes would change color.

He could daydream, but he wouldn't see the reality. He would deliver the casserole and go on about his business. Maybe he wouldn't even see Alyssa. Maybe she would have stopped at St. Anthony's or gone shopping after her shift.

He stirred the macaroni, mushroom soup, milk, and ketchup into the drained meat and thought about what he should say if he did see her. Jane was much easier. He never had to worry about what he said to her. Would he be attracted to her if she was a little less obvious, without the nose piercing and conspicuously dyed hair? If the choice were that simple, wouldn't it mean he was incredibly shallow? When he had added the cheddar cheese, green pepper, minced onion, and salt, he poured the savory mixture into a baking dish, covered it with aluminum foil, and called Jane to explain his mission.

"It sounds like you're saying goodbye," she said.

"No, but I'm paying some debts, tying up some loose ends. I still have a couple of months left on my lease."

"Did you find a job?"

"Not yet. I have an interview next week and a couple of other prospects."

"An interview? Here?"

"Santa Barbara. There are a lot of opportunities in Virginia right now, too."

"Oh, Reid! Virginia?"

"Some in Chicago too, of course, which is most likely. Anyway, when is a good time to drop by?"

****

Alyssa answered the door, which made his heart skip a beat, but Jane was right behind her. "I didn't think you'd get here so soon," Alyssa said, sounding a bit flustered.

"Oh, I drove," he explained. "I'm legal now."

"You didn't tell us," Jane cried. She gave him a congratulatory kiss, took the casserole from him, and asked, "Did you make dessert?"

"Yes, I made dessert." He held up a brown paper bag.

Jane handed Alyssa the casserole dish, took the bag, and peered inside. "Ooh!" she said, and then, "No salad?"

"Jane!" Alyssa objected. "How rude."

"You can make your own salad," Reid said. He hadn't looked directly at Alyssa yet, letting his gaze slide over her with pretended indifference. "You have plenty of time." He nodded toward the dish in her hands. "It has to bake for forty minutes. Three hundred fifty degrees. Then put the crushed potato chips— they're in the bag—on top and heat for another five minutes or so. I hope you'll like it."

"Of course we will," Jane assured him, "but it will be better with a salad. You make such wonderful salads. Pretty please?"

He shook his head, smiling. "I'm sure you can make a perfectly good salad. If you don't have the fixings, the Italian market has radicchio and whatever else you like." Jane dashed into the kitchen, and Alyssa was left to meet Reid's eyes and try to think of something to say. "Don't worry," he said, "I'm leaving."

"What?"

"I brought you a casserole. I didn't invite myself to dinner or to use your kitchen."

Jane came back with the shopping list and pen they kept on the refrigerator. "Tell me what to get," she ordered.

"Jane!" Alyssa said.

"Okay," he said, yielding with some amusement. "You can throw in anything you like, but if I was going to make a salad to go with this dish—"

"Oh, you are," Jane said confidently. "Liss can keep you company while I run to the market." When Reid didn't immediately begin to name ingredients, she thrust the list and pen at him. "I'll get my purse," she said and left the room again.

"Don't let her push you around," Alyssa advised.

He started to write and said, "I owe you an apology. I know I came on pretty strong last time I was here."

"You were in a panic because you lost your job," she said. "It's no fun getting fired."

Jane returned with her purse and held out her hand for the list as soon as he stopped writing.

"Remove the stems from the kale," he told her, "and chop it and the radicchio into bite-size pieces."

"I'm not going to do it," she said. "You are. Stay here."

"I don't think—" he began.

Jane turned at the door and ordered, "Stay."

Reid looked at Alyssa. She was wearing a pretty white V-neck blouse and pink lipstick, and her hair was brushed and shining. Had she made that effort for him? "Yes," she said, with a hint of an emotion he couldn't identify. "Stay."

"If you're sure…"

"Yes," she said and added briskly, "Don't get any

ideas."

"Do you honestly think that's all I want from you?" he asked. He spread his hands in a gesture of appeal.

"No, you want my soul. But it seems to be all I want from you. Pathetic, huh? You're not even my type."

"What is your type? Somebody like Paul Knight?"

"I guess it's silly, isn't it? To think I even have a type?" She raised the casserole dish she still held between her hands. "I guess we should preheat the oven," she said and turned away. Reid followed her into the kitchen. He headed right to the oven and turned it on while she set the dish on the counter where Jane had left the dessert bag. "You know Jane left us alone on purpose?" she asked.

"I guess she thinks we have something to say to each other," he said. He took a deep breath. "You said you couldn't have another relationship until you know what went wrong with the last one. Want me to tell you?"

"Yeah," she scoffed. "Like you're a big expert on the subject. Have you ever had a successful relationship?"

He didn't have an answer.

"You were only interested in me because I played hard to get, which you should maybe try yourself sometime, you know, instead of getting all gooey at first sight of a married woman. The wife who left her husband for you and then decided she didn't want to be married? I bet what actually happened is you lost interest. When will you lose interest in me? When my divorce is final? If I let myself fall in love with you..."

"Oh, God," Reid said. The words were so heartfelt

he hoped she would let the profanity pass. "Alyssa," he said. "You're afraid, and it's my fault, but I love you."

"No, you don't," she said angrily. "Don't say that." She sounded agitated, almost panicked.

"You asked me before if Sarah was the love of my life. I don't think I loved her at all. I wanted her, probably because I couldn't have her. You're the love of my life."

She made a sharp gesture with one hand to ward him off. "Don't! I mean really, what are you trying to pull here? You don't know how to love… Men never do."

He shook his head. "What did they do to you to make you think so?"

He couldn't mistake the emotion that welled in her eyes. Of course, he had no right to judge Paul or her father, but all she could say was, "Only mothers love you unconditionally." Her voice quavered, and she teared up.

"I know the feeling," he said softly. He hesitated, unsure how she would react, and then put his arms around her.

There was nothing sexual in his comforting embrace, but as soon as she could master her emotions, she broke away and brushed impatiently at the tears. "Sorry," she said.

"Oh, God," he said again.

"Stop that!"

"I can't help what I feel," he said. "I love you, and you don't want me. Okay, I get it. Our timing is off, to say the least. I need to go back to Chicago. It's not like I'm not used to rejection."

"So this is right in your comfort zone? I don't

believe you."

He shrugged.

"Then why does this feel like the worst thing I've ever done? You are such a nice guy, and I didn't want to hurt you."

He gave her an ironic smile. "If this is the worst thing you've ever done, you're a rank amateur."

"Oh, yeah? What's the worst thing you've ever done?"

"Besides getting two people killed?"

"Oh, Reid. It wasn't your fault."

"It was very much my fault. I'm only now realizing how much."

"Oldham is a psycho. That's not on you."

"Yes, it is. I have to live with it, and nothing you say can change it." Even as he spoke, Reid recognized a disconnect between what he said, coolly, dispassionately, taking responsibility, and what he felt. He had shut a part of himself down to keep from feeling. Survivor's guilt was a concept, a story he had told himself. He couldn't feel Alyssa's pain. He couldn't even feel his own.

"You'll always be in love with Sarah," she said. She took a step back, distancing herself from him. "The one who got away—nobody can compete with a ghost."

He shook his head. "Sarah was a fantasy. You're the real deal. But...y'know, it is what it is." He shrugged, resigned.

Alyssa studied him for a long time before she spoke again. "So...you think you know what went wrong in my last relationship?"

"Yes. He was the wrong guy. He wasn't good enough for you."

She started to protest, maybe to defend her ex, but she stopped herself. She was so beautiful like this, troubled, vulnerable, teardrops lingering on her eyelashes, but still strong, still very much the woman he wanted in his life. "No," she said, and her lips curved into a faint smile. "He wasn't."

"Neither am I," he said. "So, there you go. I can leave now if you want. You can tell Jane I had to…whatever."

She shook her head. "Stay," she said again, and her grave eyes softened. How he would like to believe she meant she wanted him to stay in Carroll City and in her life, not just for dinner. "Make Jane a wonderful salad and share this with us." She tapped the casserole. "It looks like enough for three."

"It's four servings," he admitted. He always liked to allow for leftovers, and it was easier to cook a full recipe.

"What's for dessert?" she asked. She was very much in control now, impersonal and efficient. She reached into the bag, pulled out the clear plastic container, and gasped.

"Chocolate fudge cheesecake. I made it myself."

"Of course you did. With raspberries on top. Oh, you are so bad." Her face lit up with the first real smile he had seen in a long time. "The way to a woman's heart is always through chocolate."

"Yeah?" He grinned back.

"Doesn't get you in her pants," she qualified.

He didn't want to think about making love to her. He wanted to keep her in this casual, friendly mood, the only one she was comfortable with. He took the cheesecake from her and put it in the refrigerator. "So how was work today?" he asked.

She waved a dismissive hand. "The usual," she said, and then began telling him all the ways it wasn't. The narrative could have been a downer if she'd had a rough day, but it was only rich in the variety of human folly. He was amazed she could do this kind of work and like doing it, but she would be equally mystified by his job—when he'd had one. While he listened, he glanced at his watch, decided the oven was hot enough, and put the casserole dish in.

She told him about the little girl who had followed her around, awestruck, while she made a cursory search of a burglarized home, asking, "Are you a *girl*? Can girls be p'lice?" She described the reaction of the burglar found hiding nearby, chagrined to discover he could actually be caught. The casual way she spoke of her partner, Ty, made it clear he would never be a romantic interest. Reid felt sorry for Ty, whether or not he was oblivious to her charms.

She was telling him about a routine traffic stop, enlivened by the bizarre collection of items the driver had hanging in his back window, when Jane opened the front door. She made a lot of noise, as if to warn them if they were in the middle of anything private. She marched into the kitchen, triumphantly pulled one item at a time out of a paper sack with *Gregorio's Italian Market* printed on it, and checked them off against her list.

"Did I do good?" she asked cheekily.

"You did great," he said.

"What is pecorino anyway?" she asked, but the question was only a distraction. She scrutinized Alyssa for a clue to how things stood between them now.

Nowhere, he could have told her.

"It's made from sheep's milk," he said and took the kale to the sink to wash it.

"Like baa?" Jane asked, wide-eyed.

"Is there another kind? Don't worry. You'll like it. Could you find me a large bowl?"

"How large?" she asked.

Alyssa, shaking her head, opened a cupboard and handed him a bowl of the perfect size. "Don't play dumb," she advised Jane. "He'll think you were raised in a barn."

"I think if she was raised in a barn, she would know all about sheep," Reid said. "Where *were* you raised, Jane?"

"Tennessee," she said, falling easily into a southern accent.

"Whoa," he said. "You're even farther from home than I am."

"Tennessee is where I come from," she corrected, still in a lazy twang. "It ain't home. Only a stick-in-the-mud like Liss stays in one place forever."

Reid glanced at Alyssa, who was standing close, leaning against the counter. He had his hands full of wet leafy vegetables, but he leaned over and kissed her full on the lips. "But she's the girl of my dreams," he said, trying to sound as if he was at least half joking.

She blushed a little and wiped her mouth with the back of her hand. "Don't be corny," she said, but she was smiling.

This was a way they could be together as friends, for him to flirt with her without letting himself be taken too seriously. It was not what he wanted, but maybe it would get him through the next few months.

"I hope you take the job in Santa Barbara," Jane said. "At least you can visit us sometimes."

"Cook for us, you mean," Alyssa said. "You are such a moocher, Jane."

"I promised Alyssa barbecue for her birthday," he said, "and I'd come back from Santa Barbara for that. When's *your* birthday, Jane?"

"January twelfth. You just missed it."

He wouldn't come back to Carroll City for her birthday, but if he happened to be here—"Okay, not barbecue season, but—"

"This is Southern California, silly," Jane reminded him. "It's almost always barbecue weather. What will you make for me?"

She liked to talk about food almost as much as she liked eating, and he obliged her with a fantasy menu. "Chicken Sorrento, browned in butter, with a citrus honey glaze. A pasta salad—penne, I think, with olives, tomatoes, Mozzarella cheese, basil—yes?" She had seated herself at the kitchen table, but she hung on every word. "Bread—toasted Italian?"

"Can I have biscuits instead?" she asked. She propped one elbow on the table and rested her chin on her hand.

"Buttermilk biscuits slathered in sweet butter. Does the cake have to be chocolate? I make a mean hazelnut cake."

"Ooh. Tell me more."

Reid described his recipe while he put together the salad. This was how he would get through this meal with a modicum of grace—concentrate on Jane, treat her like the child she was, and pretend Alyssa wasn't breaking his heart.

****

Alyssa was loading the dishwasher and trying not to think about Reid, but her roommate wouldn't shut up about him. "So, I guess he's going back to Chicago." Jane sighed.

"Probably. He asked me to go with him," she confessed.

"And like a dope, you said no. He asked me too, actually."

"He did?" She tried not to take it seriously, but she minded more than she could have admitted.

"He's a very sweet guy, y'know, Liss. If you married him, you'd never have to cook a day in your life. I mean, he puts pecans in his grilled cheese sandwiches."

Yes, she had seen his skill in the kitchen. She liked his hands, his strong wrists and his deft fingers with their blunt nails, and she knew what else they could do. "And the sex…" A flush of heat threatened in her face and neck.

"Whoa!" Jane exclaimed. "Say what? I thought you were taking it slow. Oh, you good little Catholic girls."

"I didn't say…" Alyssa began, still trying not to blush.

"He wouldn't with me, you know, so I thought maybe he had a problem. I guess you were the problem."

She was. She was a problem to him, and to herself. She had cried in front of him, and she hated it, hated the loss of control, hated him for seeing her tears and for the compassion and understanding she could see in his eyes. Why could she keep her emotions in check on the streets, while she dealt with every kind of horror, only to fall apart in front of this man, with whom she had so much needed to keep her dignity?

"There's no problem," she said coolly. "I'm not in love with Reid, and he's going back to Chicago, so that's the end of it. When I'm ready to date, I'll look for someone with the qualities I want in a husband. It won't be an agnostic software designer with a few culinary skills."

"Oh, you are such a snob," Jane said and left the kitchen, shaking her head.

****

On Friday Reid took Alyssa dancing again. It was the first time he drove with her in the car. At first, he was as nervous as he had been when he took the driver's license test at sixteen, as if she was likely to issue him a citation for a minor traffic violation. In fact, she didn't seem aware of his driving at all.

She wore a pale pink dress, a necklace of silver beads, and her hair in a French braid, and she looked as fetching as she always did. He was careful to keep things casual, to show her she had nothing to fear from him. He even encouraged her to accept when another man asked her to dance. He sipped a virgin piña colada while she turned smoothly and chatted politely with the stranger.

When the hand around her waist slipped too low, she dragged it back. When it happened again, she ended the dance. "Men," she said when she had stalked back to the table. "If I'd wanted to have sex with him, I would have taken him to bed."

"I'm glad you didn't. Do you ever play the cop card? Tell them you're a police officer so they won't

208

mess with you?"

She raised her eyebrows. "You think people don't want to mess with police officers?"

"I know I don't," he said. "You're the first one I've met who didn't scare me. On second thought…"

"At least you never asked me to fix a ticket. I get that a lot. I couldn't even if I wanted to, and I've never seen a reason why I would."

"You're a hard-hearted woman," he said. He was teasing and hoped she knew it.

"Yeah," she said, "and don't you forget it."

Chapter Twenty

The wheels of justice did indeed grind slowly, as Detective Cartwright had told Reid, and Facenda still languished in the county jail, waiting for his plea deal to be finalized, while the homicide detectives sought to tie him to Baird's death. He had no alibi but couldn't be placed at the scene on the night of the murder, and they had no conclusive physical evidence. Everyone was sure he had done it, but grounds for conviction still proved so elusive no case could be filed.

A polite young woman from the DA's office called Reid, introduced herself as a victim's advocate, and asked if he wanted to make an impact statement to be part of the pre-sentencing report or to speak at the upcoming sentencing hearing. He said no but asked to be notified when it was scheduled.

When the fateful Monday morning finally arrived, he went to court in his best suit. The door of the assigned courtroom stood open, but he was unsure if he should go in. While he hesitated, Detective Cartwright came down the hall and stopped to speak to him. They stood together in the hall and chatted about the weather—a surprisingly popular topic in a city where there was none to speak of.

"We're going to get this guy for homicide too," she said, grim but confident. "It all hinges on identifying the fingerprints in the office. Detective Macias is concentrating on Facenda's associates because he thinks they belong to an accomplice. I'm working Baird's—hoping it's a witness who hasn't wanted to come forward. Either way, we're pretty sure someone else was at Conavard the night of the murder."

"What if he didn't do it?" Reid asked. "What if the prints belong to the real killer, and it has nothing to do with him?"

"All the more reason to identify them, and we are pursuing other possibilities too, of course. Someone acting on behalf of the widow, whose alibi is a bit too convenient, a business rival, or somebody he met at the gay bar he liked."

Reid glanced around to be sure Mrs. Baird wasn't within earshot before he asked, "You think he was gay?"

"More like on the down low, you know, straight guys who like a little something extra on the side. If that was the motive, someone might have seen you with him at the bar and been jealous, which would explain why your picture was found with the murder weapon. But I don't believe in coincidences. Facenda tries to kill one Conavard associate and has no alibi for another? Unfortunately, it's not enough to take to a jury."

"Detective Macias doesn't believe in coincidences either," he said. "That's why he thought I did it."

"Did you?" she asked.

He hoped she was joking. "No, and I don't know who did."

"You don't think Facenda is the killer?"

"I'll leave crime solving to the experts."

"We'd appreciate that," she said, smiling.

"If he had an accomplice…"

"Watch your back," she advised, patted his arm, and headed in to find a seat.

He followed her in and sat across the aisle from Gloria Baird. She wore black, appropriate for a grieving widow, but her outfit included very tight pants, four-inch heels, considerable cleavage, and a short jacket with three-quarter sleeves. Her hair, as dark as Alyssa's but not as pretty, swooped across one eye, and her lipstick was very red. She gave him a devastatingly accusing look when he first sat down, and he went hot with shame. Randy Goff was sitting next to her but didn't glance in his direction at all.

When Facenda was escorted in, handcuffed but not shackled, in a green shirt and pants that resembled surgical scrubs, Reid felt nothing. Facenda appeared indifferent, even bored. He murmured to his public defender and glanced around the courtroom. His gaze lingered appreciatively on Mrs. Baird, who sat with her head lowered, a handkerchief to her lips. When he saw Reid, he seemed unable to identify him at first, and then he gave him a small, chilling smile. *You're dead, motherfucker.*

Reid lost interest in impact statements, pre-sentencing reports, defense and prosecution arguments, whatever Facenda might have to say for himself, and even the judge's ruling. The proceedings hadn't been called to order yet, and nobody noticed when he rose and went out. He was in enough of a hurry to nearly collide with a thin, nervous young man who was headed for the courtroom. He was vaguely familiar, but Reid couldn't identify him as anyone connected to the case. He was too upset to think straight and might not have recognized anyone. He spent five minutes in the men's room before he left the courthouse.

He didn't want to feel what he was feeling. He didn't want to be afraid of a man who would be locked away for at least the next few years. He was certain Facenda and Freddy Oldham would be closely watched in prison to prevent them from soliciting another murder attempt. Oldham had not yet been charged with attempted murder for hire, but his twenty-year Illinois sentence for Sarah's murder would certainly not be the end of his punishment. He was currently in the secure housing unit and had lost his mail and phone privileges. Reid was safe, as safe as anyone else in this dangerous world, and what happened to his assailant was nothing to him.

He was still shaken, though. Why had Facenda smiled? Shouldn't he have eyed him with hate or anger or loathing or even contempt? What did the smile mean? What did Facenda know that he didn't? Did he know how unnerved Reid would be? What if Macias was right and the other person at Conavard the night of the murder was an accomplice? Would he try again, just when Reid believed the danger was over?

He took off his jacket and tie so he wouldn't look as if he belonged at a funeral and drove to the Country Market. He wanted a cooking project that would take hours, maybe all day. He wanted the oven to be on, heating the kitchen as the California sun warmed the air outside. He would invite Alyssa and Jane to dinner or take food to them or the Halvorsens or his third-floor neighbor, Mrs. Watson, who had given him his sourdough starter.

He browsed the produce aisles, savoring the weight and texture of ripe fruits and vegetables. These easy, commonplace actions were calming, soothing. He had some of what he needed, but he filled a shopping cart with onions, avocados, apples, limes, Boston lettuce, cilantro, and sage, added a jug of apple cider, and headed for the meat counter. This was his favorite Carroll City grocery store, one with an old-fashioned butcher who could give him exactly what he wanted— no prepackaged cuts of meat here. He ordered a three-pound tenderloin which the butcher trimmed perfectly. Aside from a few sips of white wine with Alyssa on the memorable day when she served Paul Knight with divorce papers, he had not had any alcohol since the ill-fated drink with Victor Baird, but today he put a six pack of Estrella Damm in the cart.

He had already prepared sourdough before court, so it would have all day to rise. He called Alyssa's number, but her phone was apparently turned off. She would be on the job. He didn't try Jane. He made a sandwich for lunch and perused job opportunities online. He concentrated not on Chicago or Carroll City, but on other places, other states. He wanted to go where he couldn't be found by anyone associated with Oldham or Facenda. The quest occupied him until it was time to prepare the roast.

He made a paste from an apple slice with olive oil, garlic, onion, sage, rosemary, thyme, salt, and pepper and rubbed the roast with it. His efforts worked exactly the magic he had wanted. The oven warmed the kitchen on preheat, while the simple and creative tasks eased his mind.

He dressed the roast with the remaining apple, onion, garlic, and seasonings and filled the bottom of the pan with apple cider. The oven was hot enough now, and he put foil around the roast and put it in.

He had just rolled and basted it for the second time when the doorbell rang. He used the peephole because it had become a habit and was pleasantly surprised to find Alyssa standing in the hall. He opened the door quickly and said, "Hi."

"Hi," she said. "Are you okay?"

"I'm fine." He remembered how he had wished she, instead of Jane, had come to be with him after he was attacked, and here she was. She wore blue jeans and her *Zombie Apocalypse Running Team* T-shirt, but her hair was still in a tight coil at the back of her neck.

"You're cooking again," she said, although she couldn't have smelled much yet.

"I have an apple cider roast in the oven. I was going to invite you and Jane for dinner, but I couldn't reach you. Obviously, I'm glad to see you, but…why are you here?"

"I heard you didn't stay for the sentencing."

"Oh, that." Who had told her? Detective Cartwright?

"Why did you leave?"

"I don't know. I got creeped out or something." He shrugged as if it didn't matter.

"Well, I thought you might like to know what happened. Did anybody call you?"

"No. Should they have?" He gestured for her to follow him into the kitchen.

"It would have been courteous for the DA's office… Anyway, Facenda got ten years."

Reid was glad he couldn't get out any time soon, but he didn't want to think about whether ten years was appropriate for a crime that had left him with nothing broken or visibly scarred. Of course, the intent had been to kill him…

Alyssa frowned. "Are you all right?" she asked.

"Yeah. Glad it's over." Was it? "So…will you stay for dinner? Call Jane to join us?"

"Why are you making so much food?"

"I don't know. I guess it's therapeutic, especially when one of you ladies shows up to help me eat it." He consulted his watch. "You came straight from work? You can go home first if you want. Dinner won't be ready for a long time yet."

"I'm okay."

"Take a load off." He indicated the chair nearest his workspace.

She sat, drummed her fingers on the table, and asked, "Are there any more husbands who might be out to get you?"

"No, I don't think so. I just hope Oldham is done with me. How about you? Has Knight given you any more trouble?"

"No. He signed the papers and sent them back with a nasty letter. That's how my marriage ends." Everything about her had become softer, her police persona slipping away. While he checked to see how the bread dough was rising, she called Jane and left a message.

"Do you have to work tomorrow?" he asked. She was usually off Tuesday and Wednesday, but her schedule could vary.

"Nope. Two days off and then I'll work the second shift for at least the next two weeks."

"Wanna do something with me tomorrow?"

"Like what?" She regarded him with more

suspicion than curiosity.

"I don't know. Whatever you'd like."

"Thanks," she said, "but I told my dad I'd stay with my mom while he takes a day off." He would have liked to say he would go with her, but he had pushed too hard already. He needed to let her draw boundaries and be grateful she was here with him now. He wouldn't ask about Wednesday. If she wanted to spend time with him, she would suggest it.

Her phone chimed. "Jane," she said and, even as she invited her to dinner, rose and walked out of the room. What didn't she want him to hear?When she came back, she said, "She has a date, but she wants leftovers. She's been seeing a lot of the same guy lately," she added thoughtfully.

"Is he okay?" He liked Jane enough to feel protective.

"I think so. He's several years older than she is, but he seems nice. I think she might be getting ready to settle down."

"Are you?" he couldn't help asking.

"No."

"What will you do if she… I mean, will you get a smaller apartment or another roommate?"

"I don't want another roommate. Nobody else would be as easy to live with as Jane."

"How about me?"

"Get real."

So easily dismissed, he concentrated on unloading the dishwasher. "So, what will you do?"

"It's too soon to worry about it."

When nothing immediate could occupy him in the kitchen, he suggested they go out and sit on the balcony to talk. It was cooling off outside, but still very pleasant. The sun was low in the sky, but far from setting. "It is a lovely view," Alyssa said, sitting back in a cushioned teak patio chair. This was a new kind of pleasure, one of many he would like to share with her, if only she felt the way he did or anything like it. "What is Chicago like this time of year?" she asked.

"Warmer than this," he said, "and a little cooler at night. The Blues Festival is coming up."

"Is that a big deal?"

"Oh, yeah. Nothing like it."

"Are you homesick?"

"Not when I'm with you."

"Oh, please," she said, but she didn't sound annoyed. "The Cubs gonna do it again this year?"

"I wish."

"Have you ever been to Wrigley Field?"

"Lots of times, with my dad."

"What does he do?"

"He's a professor at the University of Chicago Divinity School."

"Whoa!" she said. "And you don't believe in God?"

"I didn't say that." He didn't believe in the version of God she prayed to, but that wasn't the same as unbelief.

"University of Chicago is what, Baptist?"

"It's non-sectarian. Courses in Judaism, Islam, everything. My dad teaches religion and literature."

"Wow. I can see why he wasn't crazy about the field you went into. Did your mom work?"

"She was a legal secretary before they got married. She always intended to go to law school after we were out of the house, but she never got around to it." Alyssa reached across the space between their chairs and took his hand. Her fingers were soft and warm in his and made it hard to think. He had forgotten he wanted to be in the hot kitchen all day. He would much prefer to be here, on the cooling balcony, as the sun dipped in the west, with her sympathetic hand in his. They had more to say to each other, not less, as time passed.

When he went in to roll and baste the roast, he turned on the stereo and cranked the volume up so they could hear the music outside. They could have their own Chicago Blues Festival.

"Lovely," she said when he reappeared.

"Alyssa…"

"What?"

"Why are you here?"

"You invited me to dinner."

"But why did you come? You could have called about Facenda's sentence."

"Why wouldn't I be here? You're smart and kind and a great cook, and we're friends. I like being with you."

"Okay. It wasn't because you thought I was depressed or something?" He didn't want to think she had come out of pity. The other possibility he was worried about was that she was here because he was still in danger. Maybe someone else was involved, and Facenda's smile meant he knew it wasn't over.

"Why would you be depressed?" she asked. "Facenda got what he deserved. I mean, I know you're out of work, but you'll find another job. If Conavard had any sense, they would hire you back."

They went back inside, and he put the potatoes,

tossed in olive oil, salt, and pepper, in the pan around the roast, now done enough to produce a mouthwatering aroma. Alyssa watched as he inverted and slashed the bread dough, set it in the pre-heated second oven, and tossed half a cup of ice cubes into the pan on the lower rack. "This is so much work," she said. "Don't you ever want to just nuke a TV dinner?"

"Um, no…do you?" He began juicing a lime for the salad dressing.

"All the time. Some of them are pretty good these days."

"If you say so."

"Don't be a snob, Mr. Super Chef."

"I'd rather make a sandwich if I'm too lazy to cook," he said. "Or order pizza." He whisked together the lime juice, olive oil, and seasonings.

"Maybe you should teach me a few things," she said. "Maybe we could cook together sometime." She was starting to sound like Jane. When he didn't answer, she asked, "Does that make you feel threatened?"

"Threatened? No."

"Have you ever cooked with a woman before?"

"Only my mother." He turned down the bread oven and started washing the lettuce.

"Am I in the way?" she asked.

"You're never in the way. Here." He handed her an avocado. "Pit and slice it."

"Don't I have to peel it?"

He looked at her, surprised. "Didn't your mother teach you how to cook? Never mind." He started to take the avocado back, but she held onto it.

"Tell me how to do it," she said. "I am a reasonably competent person."

"I'm sure you are. Slice it in half lengthwise, take out the pit, and scoop it out with a spoon. It will come out in one piece if you—"

"You're such a showoff." She did a "reasonably competent" job and then watched him lift and turn the bread onto the baking stone with the pancake turner. "Are you sure you don't want a job as a chef?"

"Positive. I wouldn't want to give up my amateur status." He finished the salad and asked, "Do you like your bread crust crispy or softer?"

"Crispy, I guess," she said, and he propped the bread oven door slightly ajar. "Wow," she said. "All this and bread made to order." By the time he had the roast and vegetables on a platter and the basting liquid simmering for gravy, the bread was ready to come out of the oven. It smelled wonderful, and the timing was perfect. Alyssa was suitably impressed and gazed at the feast on the table before her with something like reverence, but she frowned when he poured the beer. "I need to keep my wits about me with you around," she reminded him. "And I have to drive home."

"It's just beer, and if you drink too much, you can stay here. I'll sleep on the couch." She sampled the Estrella and agreed it was a suitable choice. Everything tasted fantastic to Reid, not because he appreciated his own cooking, but because he loved being alone with Alyssa and sharing a meal with her.

She liked it too. She commented on the tenderness of the meat and how fresh and hot the bread was. "You're not eating very much," she noticed. "Does spending so much time cooking it sort of spoil it for you? When I make cookies, I get bored with what goes into them and hardly eat any."

"It never bothered me," he said. He didn't explain that the joy of watching her eat distracted him from his own plate. "You make cookies?"

"Oatmeal chocolate chip. I'm a one-trick pony, and I don't do it very often. Store-bought is too easy."

After dinner, he refilled her half-empty glass, cleared the table, and loaded the dishwasher. If he had known she would be the sole beneficiary of his efforts, he would have planned a fancy chocolate dessert, but instead he whipped cream and sliced strawberries and marshmallows to make an easy five-minute dessert his mother had often made for unexpected guests.

"You know you can buy Cool Whip or the stuff in a can," Alyssa pointed out.

"You heathen," he said. "You'll taste the difference, I promise."

When she took her first spoonful, she rewarded him with a smile that made him unreasonably happy. He so loved to please her.

The sun was down now, so when they had finished dessert, he locked the balcony door and lowered the stereo volume to a level for comfortable listening in the living room. They listened and chatted for a while, and she told him about her day. "Doesn't this stuff get to you?" he asked.

"Sometimes. It still feels worth doing, though. I wish I understood what you do better, but tech talk makes my eyes glaze over. I don't have to know how things work, as long as they do."

"I could show you a few things sometime," he said, but he didn't care whether she understood, as long as she didn't try to nudge him into doing something else, the way his father did.

"You have a lot of good music," she said. She had put down her coffee cup, and he set his on the coffee table too and took her hand. The space was limited, but they slow-danced to Ray Charles and Janis Joplin. After a few dances, they sat on the couch again, and Reid put his arm around her with her head nestled against his shoulder. It felt like a date, even though she said they were just friends. She didn't object when he kissed her temple, and then somehow they were kissing intensely for minutes at a time and clung to each other almost without words in between. Just when he was sure there was no turning back, she shoved him away and rose abruptly. "I'd better go," she said.

Reid couldn't say anything for a minute and then he struggled against the need to say *Please stay*. He took a deep breath and said evenly, "I can take you home. Y'know, if you're not okay to drive." He wasn't sure she had had any more to drink than he had, but he didn't think about the possibility of another DUI charge, only about keeping her safe. He stood too but was careful not to touch her.

"I'm fine," she said.

"Famous last words."

She laughed and then sobered to say, "I'm sorry." She gave him a quick kiss of a very different kind. "Are we still friends?"

"Sure," he said, and then couldn't do anything but let her go.

Chapter Twenty-One

At seven fifteen on Thursday evening, Ty and Alyssa received a domestic violence call—a neighbor heard a couple yelling and glass breaking and became alarmed. "Oh, boy, my fave," Alyssa said. The house on James Street was a well-kept, upscale home in a nice neighborhood, not a typical setting for such calls. The car in the driveway was a Lexus. The lawn was very green and recently mowed. A jacaranda tree was visible behind an ornate gate in a five-foot wall.

The woman who answered the door was about fifty, with hair too evenly light brown to be natural. She wore a skirt, a short-sleeved cashmere pullover, and a string of pearls. She also had scratches on both arms. She welcomed them in with wide-eyed curiosity, apparently mystified as to why they had come.

Ty explained that a neighbor had called out of concern for their safety. Mrs. Ignasiak was taken aback, but quickly explained that a tray with two glasses had been accidentally dropped in the kitchen. "We did have a disagreement," she admitted, "but I'd hardly say we were yelling. I'm sorry if we disturbed anyone."

"Is your husband here, ma'am?" Alyssa asked.

"Why, no, not right now. He plays cards with his friends on Thursday nights. He left a few minutes ago."

"Is that your car in the driveway?"

"Yes, it is." She showed no signs of nervousness or

evasion, only a slight embarrassment.

Alyssa spoke softly, trying to suggest they only wanted to help. "I noticed you have some scratches on your arms," she said. "Did someone hurt you?"

"Oh, no, not at all. I'm afraid those are gardening injuries. I trimmed the climbing rose bush this afternoon, and I guess I wasn't careful enough. Stephen is always telling me I should wear a long-sleeved blouse when I garden, but it was nice and warm today, and I hated to cover up."

"Stephen is your husband?" Ty asked.

"Yes, that's right." Ty made a note, and Mrs. Ignasiak asked, "Is there anything else I can tell you?"

"I think we have what we need," Ty said. "We're sorry to disturb you. We just needed to be sure everything was okay."

"I appreciate your concern," she said politely and showed them to the door.

"If you do ever need our help, please call," Alyssa told her.

"Thank you, dear," Mrs. Ignasiak said. "I'm sorry, I mean Officer."

Outside, Ty headed for the car, but Alyssa said, "I'm not buying this."

"Why not?" he asked. "Everything seemed fine. She didn't give off any hinky vibes."

"They had a fight, and he left, and she has scratches all over her arms."

"She explained them."

"Come on, do you honestly think people who live in a house like this do their own gardening?"

"If she was being abused, she would have covered them up. We've done all we can."

"Let's at least check and see if there's a recently trimmed rose bush."

"We can't search the property," Ty said. "We don't have probable cause."

"If the husband left in his car, why isn't hers in the garage?"

Ty grinned. "She parks her car in the driveway because he's got the garage full of his crap, and you think he's lying dead on the kitchen floor?"

"Laugh if you want," she said, "but let's run the plate and see if it is her Lexus." Ty shook his head and got in the patrol car. Alyssa ran the plate. It was registered to Hannah Marie Ignasiak. "I'm going to look anyway," she said. She got out and paced back to peer over the garden wall. A nicely shaped white climbing rose bush in extravagant bloom grew under one of the side windows. She also spotted a green padded garden kneeler, more likely to be used by an older woman than by a professional gardener.

When she got back in the car, Ty didn't say a word, but he gave her a raised eyebrow. "Yeah, okay," she said grudgingly. He started the car. "I hate domestics," she said.

"Yeah, who doesn't?" he agreed.

She was still troubled. Even if they hadn't hurt each other, yelling and broken glass didn't suggest a peaceful marriage. Maybe all relationships came to this in the end. Her marriage had not been marked by physical violence, but there were things she couldn't forget or forgive.

Did she like Reid because he was such a pushover? She dismissed the idea immediately. Her response to victims of domestic violence was pity and contempt, and those were not emotions she could connect to Reid. She found a kind of safety in being with him, like going home, but she wasn't sure it was a good thing to feel. She didn't want to be lulled into a false sense of security. On the job, that could get people killed, and it could be every bit as dangerous in her personal life.

****

Alyssa called about ten o'clock and asked Reid if he would still be up if she dropped by after midnight. "I have some news about Facenda," she said. She was apparently at work and spoke briskly, impersonally.

If she was coming, of course he would be up. He didn't sleep well these days anyway. His first thought was that Facenda had escaped and knowing something of the sort was in the works had made him smile at the hearing. But if he was in danger, she would have warned him right away. "Sure," he said. He was careful to sound as calm and detached as she had. "Have you eaten?"

"Yes, we grabbed burgers."

"I'll make dessert," he said.

"Yeah, you would," she said and finally sounded like his Alyssa, not Officer Knight. "I have to go. I'll see you later."

Crown Ridge was a safe neighborhood, and he could have comfortably made a grocery store run this late, but he decided to use what he had on hand to make the dessert. He had a lot of options, as long as they included chocolate.

He happily dissolved gelatin in water in the double boiler and instant coffee powder separately in hot water and divided each into two parts. He was creating something for the woman he loved, and they had parted friends Monday night after hours together just talking. He very nearly whistled while he worked. Instead he turned on the stereo so music would be playing when she arrived.

He mixed the first portion of coffee with gelatin and sugar and the second with gelatin and condensed milk and poured them in half-inch layers into cocktail glasses, chilling between the alternating black and white layers. When the last layer was in the refrigerator, he chopped a Cadbury Royal Dark chocolate bar into small pieces and heated water in the bottom of the double boiler.

The doorbell rang. He knew who it was, but used the peephole anyway, to show her he had not forgotten her lesson. She was still in uniform and had a manila envelope, like the one that had held Facenda's confession. The uniform made him half believe she had come in an official capacity.

They kissed briefly, like friends. "Come in the kitchen and tell me everything," he said. "You're just in time." She followed him and stopped right inside the door. She unsnapped the holster and took out her service revolver. He would have taken it from her, but she turned away and put it in a drawer. It was a step in the right direction, but she still looked like a cop. She laid the envelope she carried on the table.

Reid melted the chocolate while Alyssa stood close by and watched him work. She seemed official enough to make him a little nervous, even though his conscience was clear. When he had told her she didn't scare him, he hadn't been thinking of her like this. "I guess you haven't been home," he said.

"I didn't even go inside the station," she said, "so

I'm in full gear." He gathered she didn't plan to stay long, but she hadn't said no to dessert. She didn't waste any more time before she put him at ease, but what she said was the last thing he expected. "Facenda is going to plead guilty to second degree murder with the special circumstance of murder for hire."

Reid couldn't catch his breath. "Baird?" he asked stupidly. "He did kill Baird?"

"Yup." Alyssa smiled, her face lighting up, and leaned in to give him a quick kiss, brief but much better than the one at the door. "We could take him to trial and get first degree, but with the sentence enhancement for murder for hire and the ten years for the attempt on you, not to mention the three strikes law, he'll still probably die in prison. The DA wants Mrs. Baird to sign off on the plea deal, but it's only a formality."

She had given him a lot to process. It took a minute, and then he asked, "But why would he confess?"

"Detective Cartwright found the witness who was in the office."

Reid sternly repressed what immediately came to his mind—*Oh my God*. Instead he said, "There *was* a witness?"

"Yes. So, there you go—there was no accomplice, and this guy will be locked away for at least thirty-five years. You should feel a lot safer now. What are you making?"

"Something good."

"You always do. Can I help?"

"You could take the glasses out of the refrigerator," he suggested. "And the dessert spoons are in the drawer on your right. Is it too late for you to drink coffee? We could do decaf."

"One cup would be all right," she said. She followed instructions, set the dessert glasses and spoons on the table, and then sat down and took a few sheets of paper out of the envelope. He didn't see how she could sit at all comfortably with all the equipment on her belt, but she must be used to it.

"It was nice of you to come and tell me this," he said. "You could have called or let me hear it on the news."

"I guess I wanted to see your face," she said.

When the chocolate was melted, Reid spooned it over the chilled layers, and topped each glass with a maraschino cherry. Satisfied, he put the steaming coffee cups on the table and sat across from her. "What did you bring?" he asked.

She took a spoonful of her dessert, murmured appreciatively, and slid the papers toward him. "You know I only love you for your cooking," she said. "This is seriously good."

"Thank you," he said, and began to read.

Tape Recorded Interview

Tarik Matthew Facenda /Detective Dale Macias

DM *This is Detective Macias, Carroll City Police Department. Today's date is Thursday, May 23rd. The time is 10:26 A.M. This will be a taped conversation with last name Facenda, F-A-C-E-N-D-A, first name Tarik, T-A-R-I-K, middle name Matthew, M-A-T-T-H-E-W. Date of birth 12-08-83. You know the drill, Mr. Facenda.*

TF *Yes.*

DM *Okay, we have your previous statement in which you admitted you went to 1049 Jefferson Street* *on January 21ˢᵗ of this year with the intention to murder Emerson Reid Lucas on behalf of Frederick Leighton Oldham.*

TF *Which I didn't do.*

DM *But it was your intention to do so. Is that right?*

TF *Yeah, yeah.*

DM *And how were you going to do it?*

TF *Bash his head in.*

DM *With what kind of weapon?*

TF *Tire iron. A knife is more personal, but Oldham wanted it to look like a mugging.*

DM *You had it with you?*

TF *Yes.*

DM *Okay, and you got on the elevator and didn't do the deed there. Why was that, exactly?*

TF *I told you why.*

DM *Because you had a witness?*

TF *I coulda done her too. She was only a whore, but she was kinda sexy, and I figured I could wait for Lucas to leave and follow him to where he parked. Better place to stage a mugging anyway. I was gonna kill time with the hooker while he was being interviewed, but it didn't work out, so I got off before his floor and took the stairs the rest of the way. I could see those guys were doing well for themselves—fancy suite of offices and all. So anyway, I hung around upstairs, but then Lucas didn't leave alone. This other geek was with him, all buddy buddy, blah blah blah.*

DM *That would have been Mr. Victor Baird, the owner and CEO of Conavard?*

TF *I didn't know who he was, just some geek. They went in the garage, and I followed them through the*

Employees Only door. They didn't even notice me. Seemed like the other dude was gonna walk Lucas all the way to his car, so I couldn't do it there. I seen the car, though, big fancy car, and wrote down the license plate. Sounded from the way they talked he was gonna get the job, so I figured I could go in early one day and wait for him in the parking garage. I was in no hurry. I didn't have to be back in Chicago until my meeting with my parole agent. If I had to go back a few times to get him alone, I would have. It always pays to take your time and get it right.

DM I'm sure it does. What about your job? You had to stay employed under the terms of your parole.

TF I said I had the flu.

DM So then what happened?

TF I went in on Saturday night to scope the place out.

DM That would be January 26th?

TF I think so. The restaurant was the only place open, but the security in the building is really lax, and I didn't have any trouble getting into the employee parking area, y'know, just to see if I could. I was going to cover the security cameras and come back around quitting time one day, but they didn't even have any. And damned if the Mercedes wasn't there. Only car in the part of the lot marked for the computer company. The rest were all in the restaurant part. Now, who does that? Works on a Saturday night if they don't have to? Workaholics and apple polishers. So anyway, I figured he was alone, and I went upstairs, and the door wasn't even locked. There was only one room with lights on.

DM Was the office door open?

TF About halfway.

DM *Did you see anybody inside?*

TF *No, but the light was on.*

DM *So what did you do?*

TF *I went by real casual and went in the restroom to make sure nobody else was in there. Thought if he heard me, he'd think it was the janitor or night watchman. Right after I came back out, I heard him come out of his office and stepped back in the shadows. I don't know if he heard something or maybe had to take a leak, but he went right in the men's room. I come up behind him, and he was like lost in thought; didn't even hear me. It was the easiest job I ever pulled. Wham, never knew what hit him. Bled like a motherfucker, too. I took his wallet so it would look like a robbery. Plus, I was going to send the ID to Oldham to prove I done it.*

DM *Prison guards censor the mail. Wouldn't it have incriminated you and Oldham both?*

TF *Oh, please. There are other ways to get stuff to people in prison than the US mail. What, were you born yesterday?*

DM *Go on. When did you realize you'd killed the wrong man?*

TF *Couldn't tell by looking at his face. Hair was the right color, but shorter—he could've got a haircut. One geek looks like another, especially when his head's bashed in.*

DM *Do you find this amusing, Mr. Facenda?*

TF *Yeah, maybe. You gotta laugh, the shit life hands you.*

DM *In this case, I would say you were the one handing out the shit. Mr. Baird is dead because you mistook him for somebody else. His wife is a grieving* *widow.*

TF A rich grieving widow.

DM Uh-huh. You said the light was on in his office when you came in?

TF Except I thought it was Lucas's office.

DM When you left, did you turn the light off?

TF No. It was on when I left.

DM Did you close the door into the office?

TF No.

DM Did you go inside?

TF No, man, I booked outta there.

DM Did you see or hear anyone inside the office after you had killed Baird?

TF I wasn't interested in the damn office.

DM So you had no idea Mr. Mark Enfield was inside the office, from where he saw you leave the restroom and place the bloody tire iron in your briefcase?

TF Shit, no. I would have offed the little weasel if I'd seen him. I didn't hear any voices when I went in. I coulda sworn Lucas—or whoever it was—was alone.

DM So what did you do then?

TF Went back to Chicago. Got word to Oldham what happened. Then it looks like Lucas might get blamed for offing Baird. Oldham woulda loved that, better than having him dead, even. But then Lucas was off the hook, so I come back to try again.

DM Which led to the charge of attempted murder for which you have already been sentenced.

Reid sat for a minute and absorbed what he had read. The first thing he could think of to say was, "Baird's murder was meant to look like a mugging? What was mine supposed to look like? Hit and run?"

He was immediately sorry he had said it. He didn't like to acknowledge that Facenda might have succeeded.

"Yeah," Alyssa said. "Until he pulled out the knife."

"If it was a witness in the office—if he didn't have an accomplice—why did he smile at me at the hearing?"

"He smiled at you? Probably messing with you, and of course at that point he believed he'd gotten away with murder."

"So…why was this Mark Enfield at Conavard on a Saturday night? I mean who is he?"

"Can't you guess? Baird picked him up at the Monkey Wrench. Why they'd choose to do it in his office I don't know. Baird could afford a hotel, and his wife was out of town. Maybe he wanted to show off his business. Enfield put his hands flat on the desk…well, I'll leave that to your imagination. They were apparently quiet about it or they were finished when Facenda got there. Enfield heard the noise in the restroom and saw him leave, and he turned off the lights and closed the door and left without telling anybody. He didn't leave any evidence behind, but I guess he forgot about fingerprints. He was afraid to come forward, maybe afraid Facenda would get him too or he'd be blamed or of the scandal, although who gives a shit nowadays? Anyway, he showed up at the sentencing. Maybe to make sure we had the right guy, or that he was going to be locked up, so he'd be safe."

"I know the feeling."

"Anyway, afterward he approached Mary Cartwright—he knew her because she'd been asking around at the bar."

"Did she give you this?" He indicated the confession

"No, of course not. She would never be so unprofessional."

"Oh!" Reid exclaimed as a thought struck him. "Is he a skinny little guy?"

"I don't know. I didn't see him. This is all second hand and speculation, you know, and you didn't hear it from me, and I didn't hear it from Mary. Enfield wouldn't talk to Macias," she added, sounding pleased at the thought.

"I saw someone at the hearing who looked familiar, and I didn't know why. Maybe he was at the bar when I went with Baird."

"So, this ends where it began," Alyssa commented. "Drinks with Victor Baird at the Monkey Wrench."

"Without which you and I would never have met."

"My life would have been a lot easier," she said, but she smiled to remove the sting. She put the pages back in the envelope and sat back to study him. "How's the job hunt going?" she asked.

"Slowly. Not much here."

"Don't give up," she said.

"I found a couple of good prospects in Chicago. I have an interview scheduled for next week." Maybe it was relief because the mystery was solved, or Alyssa's closeness, but he was more buzzed than he had been Monday night after drinking beer. He was a bit reckless and couldn't resist forcing the point. "You could go with me, see what it's like."

"Don't go there," she said.

"You might like it. We could…"

She put down her coffee cup, shoved her empty

dessert glass away, and stood up. "You know that isn't going to happen. Why do you keep beating your head against the same wall?"

He rose too and stood as close to her as he dared. "I love you," was all he could think of to say.

She made an impatient sound. "Even if I wanted to live with you, I can't go to Chicago. If I did, you'd expect me to stay home and have babies."

He shook his head. "I'd expect you to join the Chicago PD. I never imagined it any other way. I love *you*, not some domesticated fantasy version of you."

"I might not even be able to get on the force there. If you loved me, you'd want to stay here."

He took a deep breath. "Then, I'll stay here."

She shook her head. "You belong in Chicago."

"I belong where you are."

"I know you only push because I push back. You like the challenge, but deep down you're afraid of commitment."

"That doesn't make any sense. I'm trying to get *you* to commit. I think you're the one who's afraid. What are you afraid of?"

She took a minute to consider. "I'm afraid you'll change," she said finally, which at least meant she liked who he was now.

"I thought women liked to change guys into what they want them to be," he said.

"There's no such thing as *women*," she said impatiently. "We're all different."

"I've noticed," he said. She was certainly different from every other woman on the planet, at least to him, but hadn't she tried to change him, told him to speak up for himself more and not to take God's name in vain?

"Oh…are you afraid I'll turn into Paul Knight?"

"No," she said. Apparently, she saw the absurdity. "I'm afraid you'll break my heart."

He shook his head, but he couldn't think of a way to convince her, any promise he could make.

"How many times do we have to have this same argument? I do not want a relationship."

"I know…"

"You know, but you keep pushing."

"I can't help it."

"Yes, you can. You're always so easygoing, but your persistence is a kind of bullying too, you know."

"I would never bully you."

"No, you just moon around with your puppy-dog eyes, looking so sexy in a totally unthreatening way, and I don't understand why it seems so dangerous, but it does."

"Wow," he said. "You think I'm sexy, and that's why you *don't* want to be with me? That's…I'm baffled. Speechless."

"Good," she said. "That would be nice."

"If you honestly feel that way, I *will* go back to Chicago. I'm not sure what's there for me right now, but I guess it's time."

Alyssa touched his cheek and kissed him, a brief, melancholy kiss.

"Is this goodbye?" he asked.

"No…I don't want you to look like that. Don't be sad. Please." And then she was crying and kissing him, not passionately, but intensely, intimately. She took his face in her hands and covered it with sweet kisses. Reid wanted to take her into the bedroom, but this was not the time. He didn't want her to think it was only physical, although his desire for her was overwhelming right now.

I'll be whatever you want me to be, he thought, but said only, "Alyssa…"

She stopped abruptly and backed away from him. "I just had the strongest image of Jane talking to me," she said.

Reid also had a sense of Jane in the kitchen with them. Everything he felt about her crowded in, standing between him and Alyssa even as she tried to push them together. "What did she say?" He struggled to keep exasperation out of his voice.

She laughed shakily. "She said, 'Don't be a dope.' "

Reid laughed too—it sounded exactly like Jane— and he was sure he had her blessing as he took Alyssa in his arms and kissed her, undid her hair, and let his fingers slide through its luxurious length.

She let out her breath in a sigh of acquiescence, of surrender. "Okay," she said, "but this is the last time." He let her go only to unbuckle her belt. If it was the last time, they needed to make every second count.

He didn't even remember going into the bedroom. Undressing her was more challenging than ever before and very arousing, as if he were playing out a schoolboy fantasy. He unlaced her boots, slipped the heavy belt through the loops, unzipped her trousers, forced each button through a stiffly resisting hole, yanked the shirt free, unstrapped the Kevlar vest, lighter and softer than he expected, tried to figure out her sports bra, which had no clasp, and all the time he was kissing her with a new kind of desperation. She didn't help him; she was too busy undressing him.

They both spoke at once. Reid didn't quite hear her words as he blurted, "I'll stay here," and then registered what she had said—

"I'll go to Chicago."

Chapter Twenty-Two

Alyssa slept in Reid's arms for the first time. He could not imagine anything sweeter. He was amazingly calm and peaceful with her body nestled against his, her tousled hair falling across his chest. If he had been besotted before, now he was completely undone. This was what he had wanted for so long, all he had wanted, for her to belong to him enough, trust him enough, for this, exactly this.

When she stirred, lifted her head, and gazed at him in drowsy surprise, he said, "Go back to sleep." She touched his face and then closed her eyes. He eased out from under her, cradling her head until it was safely on the pillow. He bent to kiss her forehead, and she murmured something he didn't catch, but didn't move.

He took a quick shower and dressed and went into the kitchen. He knew exactly what he wanted to do. He had promised a long time ago to make cinnamon rolls from scratch. He would make them as decadently rich as he could while using non-stick cooking spray, skim milk, and low-fat cream cheese. He wanted her to love them, but he didn't want to fatten her up, not because he wouldn't adore her all roly poly, but because she had to keep fit for her job. He didn't want her to have to spend time at the gym when they could be together.

He couldn't help smiling as he melted butter in hot milk and stirred in maple syrup and yeast. Damn, but

241

life was good. He remembered Alyssa saying, "I'll go to Chicago," and knew how impossibly hard it had been for her to get to. She *would* go to Chicago some day. He would take her for a visit and show her everything he loved about his hometown and introduce her to his father, but he would not uproot her. He would stay here in Carroll City and learn to love the sunny weather and the ocean and the easygoing, small-town vibe of the place.

Flour and salt were next, in the mixer bowl, and then he slowly added the milk mixture at low speed, the whir of the machine loud in the early morning quiet. He had closed the bedroom door and didn't think the noise would disturb Alyssa. These were things he didn't know about her yet—how deeply she slept, which side of the bed she would prefer.

At least with Jane I have my own bedroom. Okay, he could handle separate rooms too. She didn't have to sleep with him every night to make him happier than he could ever deserve to be. He turned up the mixer speed, and the sound hummed through him like a song, like a prayer—*Dear God, please don't let me ever do anything to hurt her or disappoint her. Let me make culinary love to her every day of my life.*

He was high, and he needed to come down to earth, to be practical. She was a hardheaded, pragmatic woman. She considered romance corny or "gooey," which didn't mean she didn't like it. She liked to dance, and she liked chocolate and pepperoni pizza and tamales at Quique's. He guessed her favorite color was blue. She liked to be stroked in a certain way, the contemplation of which sent a slow flush of pleasure through him. He could almost feel her breath against his cheek. She liked to be touched a lot more than she liked being watched. Somebody had convinced her she was not beautiful.

She was on a later shift and could sleep late, and maybe he could lend her a robe and serve her breakfast in bed. He turned the sticky dough onto the floury bread board, shaped it into a ball, and put it in a greased, covered bowl in the warm oven. The filling didn't take long. He melted butter and mixed it with cinnamon, salt, and dark brown, granulated, and confectioners' sugar. Sweets for the sweet.

He took the dough out of the oven, rolled it into a rectangle, and sprinkled the sugar mixture over it. He remembered his mother doing this in the small square kitchen of the house he had grown up in. If she knew, she would be glad he was using her recipe to make breakfast for a woman he loved.

When the dough was rolled and sliced and returned to the oven to rise, he spread the classified section of the *Clarion* out on the table, even though he was too high to think about work. He would find a job here— any sort of tech job would do for now. The first listing he came across called for a master's degree—a sign of the tightness of the job market—but he circled a few for which his BS and years of experience would qualify him. Once he had a job, they could hunt for a condo. Or would she prefer a house? Would they be able to afford one here, where real estate prices were so high? He might be getting ahead of himself. She might change her mind. She might regret this, as she had on other occasions.

He took the cinnamon rolls, now puffed up to twice their size, out of the oven, turned it up to 350 degrees, and let them continue to rise while he folded the newspaper and set the table. Something a little extra was called for today, but he couldn't think of anything suitable. He wished he had a little garden on the balcony like some of the other tenants, so he could put a freshly-picked flower in a vase in the center of the table—if he had a vase. Would she find such a gesture corny?

When the oven was hot enough, he took the plastic wrap off the rolls and put them back in. As he set the timer, he heard the shower, and he immediately started to tense up. Now reality would intrude on his little fantasy. He wanted to hold onto the memory of her lying against him, all sleepy warmth. It was too late for breakfast in bed.

After he made the icing, he fried six slices of lean center-cut bacon in his cast iron pan. The sizzle and rich aroma further enhanced his euphoria. He took his time and made each one as nearly perfect as he could. Satisfied, he laid them on a paper napkin to drain, sprayed cooking spray in a non-stick pan, and turned on the coffeemaker.

The nicely browned cinnamon rolls were cooling on the rack, filling the room with their sweetness, and he had just cracked the eggs when Alyssa came in. Her expression was so serious he was sure she would shatter everything. She was in uniform, since she had nothing else, but had left the top button of her shirt undone and wasn't wearing her badge, belt, or boots. On her feet were his slightly battered slippers, too large for her, so she shuffled a little as she entered. Her hair was wet.

"Good morning," he said. In spite of his doubts, he couldn't help smiling at her.

"You need to come down to earth," she said.

"Yes," he said, laughing because he had used those very words. They were on the same wavelength. "Over easy okay?" he asked.

"Fine," she said. "Something smells great." She inhaled deeply. "Bacon, cinnamon, and coffee. You are good."

She opened the drawer with the dishtowels, where she had put her gun. He was afraid she would put it on and leave as soon as she could, as she had the first time, but it was only an instinctive check, to make sure she knew where it was.

"Are you a good shot?" he asked.

"Yeah, so don't piss me off. My dad started taking me to a shooting range when I was twelve." She sat at the table and watched him work. "Don't tell him you're not Catholic," she said. "I mean don't lie, but we'll all be happier if he assumes you are."

"Maybe I'll become Catholic," he said.

"I told you I didn't want you to change."

"I'm not changing," he said. "Maybe I'm…evolving."

She seemed doubtful, but she said, "I saw you in church that day…after you were fired."

"Let go," he corrected. "You were there?"

"Just for a minute." He decided not to say anything else on the subject. Let her believe whatever she wanted.

"I've met your dad," he said instead. "When am I going to meet your mother?"

Surprised, she ducked her head to hide whatever emotion she felt. She didn't answer. After a few seconds she got up, kissed his cheek, and leaned against his back for a moment before she stepped back to give him room to work. "I have a confession to make," she said.

"What's that?"

"I'm wearing your underwear."

He tried not to laugh. He'd bet she was a lot cuter in them than he was. "Okay," he said. "Do they fit?"

"No."

"You can borrow a pair of socks too, if you want. I guess it would be better if you kept some things here."

She studied him as if to assess his sincerity. "Okay," she said. "Compatibility test." He blinked. Unless he had misunderstood what she said before, the test was for people who were going to share living quarters, as she had with her husband and her roommate. She had said she wasn't ready to do it again. And now…?

"Alyssa…"

"If you do the cooking, I'll do the dishes, of course," she said.

Reid took a deep breath and matched her tone. He wasn't about to interrupt this fantasy. "Cooking is a pleasure for me, though. If you'd load the dishwasher, I'd empty it. That way I'd know where everything was." He had used a conditional tense, but she was using future. She meant what she was saying.

"I'll do the shopping if you want, if you give me a list. If you want to do it yourself, I'll still buy my personal stuff. I won't ask you to buy lipstick or tampons. I'll need space for my stuff in the bathroom. You can chime in any time, you know."

"I think you're doing fine," he said. He didn't know if this was a plan for when Jane moved out, but it sounded imminent. She hadn't said anything about finding a place together or wanting her own bedroom. Communication was the cornerstone of relationships, so perhaps he should ask. He didn't.

"I suppose you'll expect to have sex," she said.

"What? I…uh…"

She laughed. "I'm kidding. I wanted to see if you'd speak up for yourself. Of course, we'll make love when we're *both* in the mood. If you don't like something I do, tell me. No bearing a grudge and letting your feelings out later in horrible, sneaky, passive-aggressive ways."

"I'm not Paul Knight."

"I noticed. You don't get to tell me what to do."

"I wouldn't dream of it."

"And I won't tell you what to do."

"Yes, you will."

She gave him a disapproving frown. "If you won't stick up for yourself, you're kind of asking for it."

"It's fine if you do, but I won't always agree."

"Fair enough."

He flipped the eggs and began to ice the cinnamon rolls.

"Can I help?" she asked.

"You could pour the orange juice."

She opened the refrigerator. "Where was I?" she asked, and then continued. "I don't care if you watch sports all day, but baseball is the only one I'll watch with you. I'll root for the Cubs except when they play the Dodgers, but you'll have to find somebody else to rehash football plays with. When I work the first shift I want to shower first—unless you get a job with an earlier start time, of course. Remember to put the toilet seat down—but you do anyway. You are so civilized."

"Thank you," he said dryly. "I try." Her list was getting very long. She was pretty bossy for someone who had chafed at life with a passive-aggressive man.

"I don't have time for a hot breakfast on workdays, and you don't have to, like, pour my cereal or anything, or make me sack lunches. You wouldn't want me to forget how to fend for myself."

"Can I make you coffee every morning?"

"If you want. Especially if it smells like that. You should put in your two cents now."

"I think you're doing fine on your own."

"I was, you know, before you came along. I had Jane for company—"

"I want to go dancing," he said. "The Aurora ballroom, once a month."

"Boy, you drive a hard bargain." She smiled, teasing him.

He smiled back. She had their life together all figured out. He was blown away by the casual way she spoke of these practical details as if they were nothing, as if they were not signs of an apocalyptic change. Just like that, she was domesticated, *his*. "When did you figure this all out?" he asked.

"Oh, in the shower, or…maybe before. What's that look? What do you disagree with?"

"I think I must be dreaming," he said.

"Like you're having a nightmare?"

"Definitely not. But what if I can't find a job here?" he asked. She would not repeat her offer to go to Chicago, but it meant a lot that she had said it once.

"You will," she said confidently. "Don't give up."

Reid served the eggs, added three strips of bacon to

each plate, and put the cinnamon rolls on a platter, while Alyssa poured the coffee.

"You make the best bacon," she said as soon as she had taken a bite. "Why is bacon so good?"

It might have been a rhetorical question, but he said, "Something about a flavor element you can't find anywhere else. Something addictive."

"You would know. You read a lot, right? I didn't see very many books." She glanced around as if they might be in the kitchen but found only a few cookbooks.

"I still have some in storage, and I use the public library."

"No Kindle?"

"Not yet. I spend enough time staring at screens. I like real books."

"Me too," she said.

That might be the real compatibility test, and she had passed. "What do you like to read?" he asked.

"Fiction," she said, a bit sheepish. "I suppose you think that's dumb."

"Why? I read a lot of fiction."

"What are you reading now?"

"Gillian Flynn." She looked blank so he said, "She wrote *Gone Girl*."

"Oh, yes. I read it. It was great. I can never remember the author's name because I kept thinking it was a man. She really got into the guy's head."

"It's a pretty negative view of marriage, though."

"No more than mine," she said. She took a swig of orange juice before she added, "Funny thing for a serial cheater to say."

"Ouch."

Linda Griffin

"Sorry. Technically I guess you weren't the cheater. If I hadn't been separated, would you have…?"

"Only if you encouraged me. Which of course you didn't. I *have* learned my lesson."

She took a bite of her cinnamon roll, and her eyes widened. "Oh, Reid, these are…"

He expected her to say sinful or decadent, so he put in, "I used skim milk and low-fat cream cheese."

"Cream cheese? No wonder. They're *way* better than the refrigerator kind."

"Homemade is always better."

"Don't be smug," she said. "Anyway, what else?" They were back to the list. "We'll keep our finances separate, except where it makes sense to share."

"Maybe we should put this on paper," he suggested. "Maybe we should get married and have a pre-nup."

"Ha, ha."

"I would be corny and get down on one knee if you'd like that better."

"Don't you dare."

"What would you say?"

"No. Or yes. I don't know. I'm still sort of married. He said all the pretty words too."

"Are you going to keep his name?"

"Sharpe is a burden in its own way, on the job."

"How about Lucas?"

"No, don't go there," she said firmly. "Don't get ahead of yourself. We don't even know if this will work." She took a deep breath and went on. "I'll do the laundry, but I won't pick up after you. I'll make the bed, unless you're still in it, and clean the bathroom."

The list seemed to be endless, and none of it was

important. Only one thing mattered—she intended to belong in his life.

After breakfast, she loaded the dishwasher, as if she already lived there, and then she studied him critically and said, "You need a haircut."

"Okay." He was sure she was right—he had had only one since January.

She was still studying him. "Would you let me do it?"

"Can I trust you with a pair of scissors?"

"Do you have any?"

He opened the junk drawer—he had accumulated an astonishing amount of stuff in the last few months.

She frowned at the offered blades critically. "I guess they'll do. I'll use mine next time. Do you have an apron?"

She had him sit in a chair in the middle of the kitchen, put his barbecue apron over his clothes and a towel around his shoulders, and snipped away. The sensation made him feel both edgy and soothed. It was not the brisk business transaction it was at Supercuts, but a very sensuous, intimate act, not arousing, but satisfying in a completely different way. Locks of his hair fell on the apron and the floor, and she blew them softly off his neck. This was getting better and better. "Have you done this before?" he asked.

"Yes," she said, but she didn't elaborate.

"Did you cut your husband's hair?"

"Fat chance. Didn't you notice his perfect hair when he was here?"

"It wasn't my main focus at the time."

"He wouldn't have let me lay a finger on it. I like yours a little shaggy, but would you mind if I cut it a little bit shorter this time? It will grow back really fast if you don't like it."

"Go ahead," he said comfortably. "I'm at your mercy."

"Yes, you are. We're getting hair all over the floor. Should we have done this in the bathroom?"

"It will sweep up."

"Will you get annoyed if I'm messier than you are?"

"No, but your apartment isn't messy. Well, Jane's room…"

She stopped snipping. "You've been in her bedroom?"

"No. The door was open when I brought you the meds. Don't keep trying to make up something about me and Jane. It was always you."

"She said you asked her to go to Chicago with you."

"Uh, yeah, I guess I did."

"I'm waiting," she said.

He had no defense. He couldn't remember what his state of mind had been at the time.

"You are so busted," she said, but she laughed and tugged playfully at his hair.

"She said we both knew she wasn't the one I wanted."

She started cutting again, let a snippet fall on his nose, and blew it off, her sweet breath on his face. "Reid?"

"Yes?"

"There's something else I have to say that I didn't mention before."

"What's that?" It sounded serious, but he was too

relaxed to tense up.

She leaned in and kissed his ear. "I love you," she whispered, and as he sat in a rented kitchen with sharp scissors dangerously close, between one heartbeat and the next, Carroll City became home.

A word about the author…

Linda Griffin retired as Fiction Librarian for the San Diego Public Library to spend more time on her writing, and her work has been published in numerous journals. In addition to the three R's—reading, writing, and research—she enjoys Scrabble, movies, and travel. This is her fourth Wild Rose Press novel.

Visit her at:
http://www.lindagriffinauthor.com/

Thank you for purchasing
this publication of The Wild Rose Press, Inc.

For questions or more information
contact us at
info@thewildrosepress.com.

The Wild Rose Press, Inc.
www.thewildrosepress.com

www.ingramcontent.com/pod-product-compliance
Lightning Source LLC
Chambersburg PA
CBHW060539260626
47161CB00003B/965